The realisation cam
than Hasson might
He had already climb
cared to think abou
within him was slowly abating.

Hanging motionless in the icy blue solitude, poised on the threshold of space, Hasson gazed all about him and felt . . . *nothing*. There was no fear, no elation, no wonder, no sense of achievement, no communion with the cosmos—removed from the context of humanity he had lost his humanity.

He completed a full survey of the heavens, knew himself to be a stranger there, then adjusted a control on his belt and began the long and lonely fall to Earth.

Also by Bob Shaw in VGSF

NIGHT WALK

MEDUSA'S CHILDREN

A WREATH OF STARS
(VGSF Classic)

WHO GOES HERE?

THE SHADOW OF HEAVEN

BOB SHAW

TERMINAL VELOCITY

VGSF

VGSF is an imprint of Victor Gollancz Ltd
14 Henrietta Street, London WC2E 8QJ

First published in Great Britain 1978
by Victor Gollancz Ltd, under the title *Vertigo*

This edition first published in Great Britain 1991
by Victor Gollancz Ltd

First VGSF edition 1992

A portion of this novel first appeared in
Science Fiction Monthly under the title
'Dark Icarus'

A catalogue record for this book is available
from the British Library

ISBN 0 575 05314 3

Printed and bound in Great Britain
by Cox & Wyman Ltd, Reading

To Chris Priest – counsellor and friend

PROLOGUE

THE DEAD COP came drifting in towards the Birmingham control zone at a height of some three thousand metres. It was a winter night, and the sub-zero temperatures which prevailed at that altitude had solidified his limbs, encrusted the entire body with black frost. Blood flowing through shattered armour had frozen into the semblance of a crab, with its claws encircling his chest. The body, which was in an upright position, rocked gently on stray currents, performing a strange aerial shuffle. And at its waist a pea-sized crimson light blinked on and off, on and off, its radiance gradually fading under a thickening coat of ice.

Air Police Sergeant Robert Hasson felt more exhausted and edgy than he would have done after an eight-hour crosswind patrol. He had been in the headquarters block since lunchtime, dictating and signing reports, completing forms, trying to wrest from the cashier's office the expenses which had been due to him two months earlier. And then, just as he was about to go home in disgust, he had been summoned to Captain Nunn's office for yet another confrontation over the Welwyn Angels case. The four on remand—Joe Sullivan, Flick Bugatti, Denny Johnston and Toddy Thoms—were sitting together at one side of the office, still in their flying gear.

"I'll tell you what disturbs me most about this whole affair," Bunny Ormerod, the senior barrister, was saying with practised concern. "It is the utter indifference of the police. It is the callousness with which the tragic death of a child is accepted by the arresting officers." Ormerod moved closer to the four Angels, protectively, identifying with them. "One would think it was an everyday occurrence."

Hasson shrugged. "It is, practically."

Ormerod allowed his jaw to sag, and he turned so that the brooch recorder on his silk blouse was pointing straight at Hasson. "Would you care to repeat that statement?"

Hasson stared directly into the recorder's watchful iris. "Practically every day, or every night, some moron straps on a CG harness, goes flying around at five or six hundred kilometres an hour, thinking he's Superman, and runs into a pylon or a tower-block. And you're dead right—I don't give a damn when they smear themselves over the sides of buildings." Hasson could see Nunn becoming agitated behind his expanse of desk, but he pressed on doggedly. "It's only when they smash into other people that I get worked up. And then I go after them."

"You hunt them down."

"That's what I do."

"The way you hunted down these children."

Hasson examined the Angels coldly. "I don't see any children. The youngest in that gang is sixteen."

Ormerod directed a compassionate smile towards the four black-clad Angels. "We live in a complex and difficult world, Sergeant. Sixteen years isn't a very long time for a youngster to get to know his way around it."

"Balls," Hasson commented. He looked at the Angels again and pointed at a heavy-set, bearded youth who was sitting behind the others. "You—Toddy—come over here."

Toddy's eyes shuttled briefly. "What for?"

"I want to show Mr Ormerod your badges."

"Naw. Don't want to," Toddy said smugly. "Sides, I like it better over here."

Hasson sighed, walked to the group, caught hold of Toddy's lapel and walked back to Ormerod as if he was holding nothing but the piece of simulated leather. Behind him he heard frantic swearing and the sound of chairs falling over as Toddy was dragged through the protective screen of his companions. The opportunity to express his feelings in action, no matter how limited, gave Hasson a therapeutic satisfaction.

Nunn half rose to his feet. "What do you think you're doing, Sergeant?"

Hasson ignored him, addressing himself to Ormerod. "See this badge? The big 'F' with wings on it? Do you know what it means?"

"I'm more interested in what your extraordinary behaviour means." One of Ormerod's hands was purposely, but with every appearance of accident, blocking his recorder's field of view. Hasson knew this was because of recent legislation under which the courts refused to consider any recorded evidence unless the entire spool was presented—and Ormerod did not want a shot of the badge.

"Have a look at it." Hasson repeated his description of the badge for the benefit of the soundtrack. "It means that this quote child unquote has had sexual intercourse in free fall. And he's proud of it. Aren't you, Toddy?"

"Mister Ormerod?" Toddy's eyes were fixed pleadingly on the barrister's face.

"For your own good, Sergeant, I think you should let go of my client," Ormerod said. His slim hand was still hovering in front of the recorder.

"Certainly." Hasson snatched the recorder, plucking a hole in Ormerod's blouse as he did so, and held the little instrument in front of the Angel's array of badges. After a moment he pushed Toddy away from him and gave the recorder back to Ormerod with a flourish of mock-courtesy.

"That was a mistake, Hasson." Ormerod's aristocratic features had begun to show genuine anger. "You've made it obvious that you are taking part in a personal vendetta against my client."

Hasson laughed. "Toddy isn't your client. You were hired by Joe Sullivan's old man to get him out from under a manslaughter charge, and big simple Toddy just happens to be in the same bag."

Joe Sullivan, sitting in the centre of the other three Angels, opened his mouth to retort, but changed his mind. He appeared to have been better rehearsed than his companions.

"That's right," Hasson said to him. "Remember what you were told, Joe—let the hired mouth do all the talking." Sullivan shifted resentfully, staring down at his blue-knuckled hands, and remained silent.

"It's obvious we aren't achieving anything," Ormerod said to Nunn. "I'm going to hold a private conference with my clients."

"Do that," Hasson put in. "Tell them to peel off those badges, won't you? Next time I might pick out an even better one." He waited impassively while Ormerod and two policemen ushered the four Angels out of the room.

"I don't understand you," Nunn said as soon as they were alone. "Exactly what did you think you were doing just now? That boy has only to testify that you manhandled him . . ."

"That boy, as you call him, knows where we could find the Fireman. They all do."

"You're being too hard on them."

"You aren't." Hasson knew at once that he had gone too far, but he was too obstinate to begin retracting the words.

"What do you mean?" Nunn's mouth compressed, making him look womanly but nonetheless dangerous.

"Why do I have to talk to that load of scruff up here in your office?

What's wrong with the interview rooms downstairs? Or are they only for thugs who haven't got Sullivan money behind them?"

"Are you saying I've taken Sullivan's money?"

Hasson thought for a moment. "I don't believe you'd do that, but you let it make a difference. I tell you those four have flown with the Fireman. If I could be left alone for half an hour with any of them I'd . . ."

"You'd get yourself put away. You don't seem to understand the way things are, Hasson. You're a skycop—and that means the public doesn't want you about. A hundred years ago motorists disliked traffic cops for making them obey a few commensense rules; now everybody can fly, better than the birds, and they find this same breed of cop up there with them, spoiling it for them, and they *hate* you."

"I'm not worried."

"I don't think you're worried about police work either, Hasson. Not really. I'd say you're hooked on cloud-running every bit as much as this mythical Fireman, but you want to play a different game."

Hasson became anxious, aware that Nunn was leading up to something important. "The Fireman is real—I've seen him."

"Whether he is or not, I'm grounding you."

"You can't do that," Hasson blurted instinctively.

Nunn looked interested. "Why not?"

"Because . . ." Hasson was striving for the right words, any words, when the communicator sphere on Nunn's desk lit up redly, signalling a top priority message.

"Go ahead," Nunn said to the sphere.

"Sir, we're picking up an automatic distress call," it replied with a male voice. "Somebody drifting out of control at three thousand metres. We think it must be Inglis."

"Dead?"

"We've interrogated his compack, sir. No response."

"I see. Wait till the rush hour is over and send somebody up for him. I'll want a full report."

"Yes, sir."

"I'm going up for him now," Hasson said, moving towards the door.

"You can't go through the traffic streams at this hour." Nunn got to his feet and came around the desk. "And you're grounded. I mean that, Hasson."

Hasson paused, knowing that he had already stretched to the limit the special indulgence granted to members of the Air Patrol. "If that's Lloyd

Inglis up there, I'm going up to get him right now. And if he's dead, I'm grounding myself. Permanently. Okay?"

Nunn shook his head uncertainly. "Do you want to kill yourself?"

"Perhaps." Hasson closed the door and ran towards the tackle room.

He lifted off from the roof of the police headquarters into a sky which was ablaze with converging rivers of fire. Work-weary commuters pouring up from the south represented most of the traffic, but there were lesser tributaries flowing from many points of the compass into the vast aerial whirlpool of the Birmingham control zone. The shoulder-lights and angle-lights of thousands upon thousands of fliers shifted and shimmered, changes of parallax causing spurious waves to progress and retrogress along the glowing streams. Vertical columns of brilliance kept the opposing elements apart, creating an appearance of strict order. Hasson knew, however, that the appearance was to some extent deceptive. People who were in a hurry tended to switch off their lights to avoid detection and fly straight to where they were going, regardless of the air corridors. The chances of colliding with another illegal traveller were vanishingly small, they told themselves, but it was not only occasional salesmen late for appointments who flew wild. There were the drunks and the druggies, the antisocial, the careless, the suicidal, the thrill-seekers, the criminal—a whole spectrum of types who were unready for the responsibilities of personal flight, in whose hands a counter-gravity harness could become an instrument of death.

Hasson set his police flare units at maximum intensity. He climbed cautiously, dye gun at the ready, until the lights of the city were spread out below him in endless growing geometrics. When the information display projected on to the inner surface of his visor told him he was at a height of two hundred metres he began paying particular attention to his radar. This was the altitude at which rogue fliers were most numerous. He continued rising rapidly, controlling the unease which was a normal reaction to being suspended in a darkness from which, at any moment, other beings could come hurtling towards him at lethal velocity. The aerial river of travellers was now visible as separate laminae, uppermost levels moving fastest, which slipped over each other like luminous gauze.

A further eight hundred metres and Hasson began to relax slightly. He was turning his attention to the problem of homing in on Inglis when his proximity alarm sounded and the helmet radar flashed a bearing. Hasson twisted to face the indicated direction. The figure of a man flying without lights, angled for maximum speed, materialised in the light of Hasson's flare units. Veteran of a thousand such encounters, Hasson had time to calculate a miss distance of about ten metres. Within the fraction of a second available to him, he aimed his gun and fired off a cloud of indelible dye. The other man passed through it—glimpse of pale, elated face and dark unseeing eyes—and was gone in a noisy flurry of turbulence. Hasson called HQ and gave details of the incident, adding his opinion that the rogue flier was also guilty of drug abuse. With upwards of a million people airborne in the sector at that very moment it was unlikely that the offender would ever be caught, but his flying clothes and equipment had been permanently branded and would have to be replaced at considerable expense.

At three thousand metres Hasson switched to height maintenance power, took a direction-finder reading on Inglis's beacon and began a slow horizontal cruise, eyes probing the darkness ahead. His flares illuminated a thickening mist, placing him at the centre of a sphere of foggy radiance and making it difficult to see anything beyond. This was close to the limit for personal flying without special heaters and Hasson became aware of the cold which was pressing in on him, searching for a weakness in his defences. The traffic streams far below looked warm and safe.

A few minutes later Hasson's radar picked up an object straight ahead. He drew closer until, by flarelight, he could make out the figure of Lloyd Inglis performing its grotesque shuffle through the currents of dark air. Hasson knew at once that his friend was dead but he circled the body, keeping just outside field interference distance, until he could see the gaping hole in Inglis's chest plate. The wound looked as though it had been inflicted by a lance . . .

A week earlier Hasson and Inglis had been on routine patrol over Bedford when they detected a pack of about eight flying without lights. Inglis had loosed off a miniflare which burst just beyond the group, throwing them briefly into silhouette, and both men had glimpsed the slim outline of a lance. The transportation of any solid object by a person using a CG harness was illegal, because of the danger to other air travellers and people on the ground, and the carrying of weapons was rare even among rogue fliers. It seemed likely that they had chanced on the Fireman. Spreading their nets and snares, Hasson and Inglis had flown in pursuit. During the subsequent low-level chase two people had died—one of them a young woman, also flying without lights, who had strayed into a head-on collision with one of the gang. The other had been a pack leader who had almost cut himself in two on a radio mast. At the end of it, all the two policemen had had to show for their efforts had been four unimportant members of the Welwyn Angels. The Fireman, the lance-carrier, had got away to brood about the incident, safe in his anonymity.

Now, as he studied the frozen body of his former partner, Hasson understood that the Fireman had been inspired to revenge. His targets would have been identified for him in the news coverage given to the arrest of Joe Sullivan. Swearing in bitterness and grief. Hasson tilted his body, creating a horizontal component in the lift force exerted by his CG harness. He swooped in on the rigid corpse, locked his arms around it and, immediately, both bodies began to drop as their counter-gravity fields cancelled each other out. No stranger to free fall, Hasson efficiently attached a line to an eye on Inglis's belt and pushed the dead man away from him. As the two separated to beyond field interference distance the upward rush of air around them gradually ceased. Hasson checked his data display and saw that he had fallen little more than a hundred metres. He paid the line out from a dispenser at his waist until Inglis's body was at a convenient towing distance, then he flew west, aiming for a point at which it would be safe to descend through the commuter levels. Far beneath him the traffic of the Birmingham control zone swirled like a golden galaxy, but Hasson—at the centre of his own spherical universe of white misty light—was isolated from it, cocooned in his own thoughts.

Lloyd Inglis—the beer-drinking, book-loving spendthrift—was dead. And before him there had been Singleton, Larmor and McMeekin. Half of Hasson's original squad of seven years ago had died in the course of duty . . . and for what? It was impossible to police a human race which had been given its three-dimensional freedom with the advent of the CG harness. Putting a judo hold on gravity, turning the Earth's own attractive force back against itself, had proved to be the only way to fly. It was easy, inexpensive, exhilarating—and impossible to regulate. There were eighty million personal fliers in Britain alone, each one a superman impatient of any curb on his ability to follow the sunset around the curve of the world. Perhaps the inevitable price of freedom was a slow rain of broken bodies drifting to Earth as their powerpacks faded and . . .

The attack took Hasson by surprise.

It came so quickly that the proximity alarm and the howling of air displaced by the attacker's body were virtually simultaneous. Hasson turned, saw the black lance, jack-knifed to escape it, received a ferocious glancing blow, and was sent spinning—all in the space of a second. The drop caused by the momentary field interference had been negligible. He switched off his flares and flight lights in a reflexive action and struggled to free his arms from the towline which was being lapped around him by his own rotation. When he had managed to stabilise himself he remained perfectly still and tried to assess the situation. His right hip throbbed painfully from the impact, but as far as he could tell no bones had been broken. He wondered if his attacker was going to be content with having made a single devastating pass, or if this was the beginning of a duel.

"You were quick, Hasson," a voice called from the darkness. "Quicker than your wingman. But it won't do you any good."

"Who are you?" Hasson shouted as he looked for a radar bearing.

"You know who I am. I'm the Fireman."

"That's a song." Hasson kept his voice steady as he began spreading his snares and nets. "What's your real name? The one your area psychiatrist has on his books."

The darkness laughed. "Very good, Sergeant Hasson. Playing for time and trying to goad me and learn my name all at once."

"I don't need to play for time—I've already broadcast a QRF."

"By the time anybody gets here you'll be dead, Hasson."

"Why should I be? Why do you want to do this?"

"Why do you hunt my friends and ground them?"

"They're a menace to themselves and to everybody else."

"Only when you make them fly wild. You're kidding yourself, Hasson. You're a skycop and you like hounding people to death. I'm going to ground you for good—and those nets won't help you."

Hasson stared vainly in the direction of the voice. "Nets?"

There was another laugh and the Fireman began to sing. *"I can see you in the dark, 'cause I'm the Fireman; I can fly with you and you don't even know I'm there . . ."* The familiar words were growing louder as their source drew near, and abruptly Hasson made out the shape of a big man illuminated by the traffic streams below and by starlight from above. He looked fearsome and inhuman in his flying gear.

Hasson yearned for the firearm which was denied to him by British police tradition, and then he noticed something. "Where's the lance?"

"Who needs it? I let it go." The Fireman spread his arms and—even in the dimness, even with the lack of spatial reference points—it became apparent that he was a giant, a man who had no need of weapons other than those which nature had built into him.

Hasson thought of the heavy lance plummeting down into a crowded suburb three thousand metres below and a cryogenic hatred stole through him, reconciling him to the forthcoming struggle, regardless of its outcome. As the Fireman came closer, Hasson whirled a net in slow circles, tilting his harness to counteract the spin the net tried to impart to him. He raised his legs in readiness to kick, and at the same time finished straightening out the towline which made Inglis's body a ghastly spectator to the event. He felt nervous and keyed up, but not particularly afraid now that the Fireman had discarded his lance. Aerial combat was not a matter of instinct, it was something which had to be learned and practised, and therefore the professional always had the edge on the amateur, no matter how gifted or strongly motivated the latter might be. For example, the Fireman had made a serious mistake in allowing Hasson to get his legs fully drawn up into the position from which the power of his thighs could be released in an explosive kick.

Unaware of his blunder, the Fireman edged in slowly, vectoring the lift of his harness with barely perceptible shoulder movements. *He's a good flier*, Hasson thought, *even if he isn't so good on combat theory and . . .*

The Fireman came in fast—but not nearly as fast as he should have done. Hasson experienced something like a sense of luxury as he found himself with time to place his kick exactly where he wanted it. He chose the vulnerable point just below the visor, compensated for the abrupt drop which occurred as both CG fields cancelled out, and unleashed enough energy to snap a man's neck. Somehow the Fireman got his head out of the way in time and caught hold of Hasson's outstretched leg. Both men were falling now, but at an unequal rate because Hasson was tethered to Inglis whose CG field was too far away to have been cancelled. In the second before they parted, the Fireman applied the leverage of his massive arms and broke Hasson's leg sideways at the knee.

Pain and shock obliterated Hasson's mind, gutting him of all strength and resolve. He floated in the blackness for an indeterminate period, arms moving uncertainly, face contorted in a silent scream. The great spiral nebula far below continued to spin, but a dark shape was moving steadily across it, and part of Hasson's mind informed him that there was no time for indulgence in natural reactions to injury. He was hopelessly out-classed on the physical level, and if life were to continue it would only be through the exercise of intelligence. But how was he to think when pain had invaded his body like an army and was firing mortar shells of agony straight into his brain?

For a start, Hasson told himself, *you have to get rid of Lloyd Inglis*. He began reeling in his comrade's body with the intention of unhooking it, but almost immediately the Fireman spoke from close behind him.

"How did you like it, Hasson?" The voice was triumphant. "That was to show you I can beat you at your own game. Now we're going to play my game."

Hasson tried drawing the line in faster. Inglis's body bobbed closer and finally came within interference radius. Hasson and Inglis began to fall. The Fireman dived in on them on the instant, hooked an arm around Hasson's body, and all three dropped together. The whirlpool of fire began to expand beneath them.

"This is *my* game," the Fireman sang through the gathering slipstream. *"I can ride you all the way to the ground, 'cause I'm the Fireman."*

Hasson, knowing the tactics of aerial chicken, shut out the pain from his trailing leg, reached for his master switch, but hesitated without throwing it. In two-man chicken the extinguishing of one CG field restored the other one to its normal efficacy, causing a fierce differential which tended to drag one opponent vertically away from the other. The standard counter-move was for the second man to kill his own field at the same time so that both bodies would continue to plunge downwards together until somebody's nerve broke and forced him to re-activate his harness. In the present game of death, however, the situation was complicated by the presence of Inglis, the silent partner who had already lost. His field would continue negating those of the other two, regardless of what they did, unless . . .

Hasson freed an arm from the Fireman's mock-sexual embrace and pulled Inglis's body in close. He groped for the dead man's master switch but found only a smooth plaque of frozen blood. The jewelled horizons were rising rapidly on all sides now, and the circling traffic stream was opening like a carnivorous flower. Air rushed by at terminal velocity, deafeningly. Hasson fought to break the icy casting away from the switch on Inglis's harness, but at that moment the Fireman slid an arm around his neck and pulled his head back.

"Don't try to get away from me," he shouted into Hasson's ear. "Don't try to chicken out—I want to see how well you bounce."

They continued to fall.

Hasson, encumbered by his nets, felt for the buckle of the belt which held, among other things, the towline dispenser. He fumbled it open with numb fingers and was about to release Inglis's body when it occurred to him he would gain very little in doing so. An experienced chicken player always delayed breaking out of field interference until the last possible instant, leaving it so late that even with his harness set at maximum lift he hit the ground at the highest speed he could withstand. The Fireman probably intended going to the limit this time, leaving Hasson too disabled to prevent himself being smashed on impact. Getting rid of Inglis's body would not change that.

They had dropped almost two thousand metres and in just a few seconds would be penetrating the crowded commuter levels. The Fireman began to whoop with excitement, grinding himself against Hasson like a rutting dog. Holding Inglis with his left hand, Hasson used his right to loop the plasteel towline around the Fireman's upraised thigh and to pull it into a hard knot. He was still tightening the knot as they bombed down into the traffic flow. Lights flashed past nearby and suddenly the slow-spinning galaxy was above them. Patterns of street lamps blossomed beneath, with moving ground cars clearly visible. This, Hasson knew, was close to the moment at which the Fireman had to break free if he was to shed enough downward velocity before reaching ground level.

"Thanks for the ride," the Fireman shouted, his voice ripping away in the slipstream. "Got to leave you soon."

Hasson switched on his flares and then jerked the towline violently, bringing it to the Fireman's attention. The Fireman looked at the loop around his thigh. His body convulsed with shock as he made the discovery that it was he and not Hasson who was linked to the dead and deadly skycop. He pushed Hasson away and began clawing at the line. Hasson swam free in the wind, knowing that the line would resist even the Fireman's great strength. As he felt his CG field spread its invisible wings he turned to look back. He saw the two bodies, one of them struggling frantically, pass beyond the range of his flares on their way to a lethal impact with the ground.

Hasson had no time to waste in introspection—his own crash landing was about to occur and it would require all his skill and experience to get him through it alive—but he was relieved to find that he could derive no satisfaction from the Fireman's death. Nunn and the others were wrong about him.

Even so, he thought, during the final hurtling seconds, *I've hunted like a hawk for far too long. This is my last flight.*

He prepared himself, unafraid, for the earth's blind embrace.

CHAPTER 1

THE DRIVE TO Chivenor had been long and tiring. As it had progressed the pain in Hasson's back had grown worse, and with the pain had come a steady deterioration of his mood. At first there had been stray misgivings, hints of sadness which anybody might have felt on passing through a series of towns and villages where all commerce and community life seemed to have been vanquished by the chill grey rains of March. By the time they had reached the north Devon coast, however, Hasson felt more than normally dejected, and later when the car surmounted a rise—giving its three occupants a glimpse of the Taw estuary—he realised he was terrified of the journey that lay ahead.

How can this be? he thought, unable to reconcile his feelings with those he would have experienced six weeks earlier in similar circumstances. *I'm being given a free trip to Canada, three months' leave on full pay, all the time I need to rest and recuperate . . .*

"I always think there's something *right* about the principle of the flying boat," said Colebrook, the police surgeon, who was sitting in the rear seat with Hasson. "The whole idea of flying over the sea in ships, having four-fifths of the globe for a landing place . . . It all seems natural, if you know what I mean—technology and nature going hand-in-hand."

Hasson nodded. "I see what you're getting at."

"Just *look* at those things." A gesture of Colebrook's plump, strong hand took in the slate-blue strip of water and the apparently haphazard scattering of flying boats. "Silver birds, as our Polynesian cousins might say. Do you know why they aren't painted?"

Hasson shook his head, trying to take an interest in the surgeon's conversation. "Can't think."

"The load factor. Economics. The weight of the paint would be equal to the weight of an extra passenger."

"Is that right?" Hasson smiled, hopelessly, and saw the boyish enthusiasm fade from Colebrook's face to be replaced by a look of professional concern. He cursed himself for not having made a greater effort to cover up.

"Problems, Rob?" Colebrook turned bodily to get a better look at his patient, pulling his suit into silky diagonal folds across his stomach. "How do you feel?"

"A bit tired that's all. A few aches and pains. I'll hang together."

"I'm not asking about that side of it. Have you taken any Serenix today?"

"Well . . . " Hasson abandoned the attempt to lie. "I don't like taking pills."

"What's that got to do with anything," Colebrook said impatiently. "I don't like brushing my teeth, but if I stop the result will be a lot of pain and a mouth full of delph—so I brush my teeth."

"It's hardly the same thing," Hasson protested.

"It's *exactly* the same thing, man. Your nervous system is bound to give you hell for a month or two, maybe longer, but the fact that a thing is natural doesn't mean you have to put up with it. There aren't any medals for this, Rob—no Misery Cross or Depression Diploma . . ."

Hasson raised a finger. "That's good, doc. I like that."

"Swallow a couple of those caps, Rob. Don't be a fool." Colebrook, who had too much medical experience to allow himself to be upset by a wayward patient, leaned forward and tapped Air Police Captain Nunn on the shoulder, his expansive mood returning. "Why don't we all go to Canada, Wilbur? We could all do with a break."

Nunn had been at the wheel most of the way from Coventry and was showing signs of strain. "Some of us can't be spared," he said, refusing to be captivated by pleasantries. "Anyway, it's too early in the year for me. I'd rather wait till the Iceland-Greenland corridor is cleared."

"That could take months."

"I know, but some of us can't be spared." Nunn transferred the weight of his forearms on to the steering wheel, managing to convey his disinclination to talk. The sky ahead had cleared to an antiseptic pale blue, but the ground was still wet, and the car's wheels made swishing sounds on the tarmac curves as it descended towards the airfield and flying boat terminal at Chivenor. Nunn continued to drive fast, with broody concentration, as the view of the estuary was lost behind a row of dripping evergreens.

Hasson, slouched uncomfortably in the rear seat, stared at the back of his chief's neck and wished there had been no reference to the clearing of the flight corridors. His plane was due to take off in little more than an hour and the last thing he wanted was to think about the possibility of it smashing into any human bodies which might be drifting through the low cloud and fog that often obscured the Atlantic air lines.

Nobody in the west had any clear idea of what was going on in the vast tracts of land spanning the eastern hemisphere from the Zemlayas to Siberia, but each winter a sparse, slow blizzard of frozen bodies—kept aloft by their CG harnesses—came swirling down over the pole, endangering air cargo traffic between Britain and North America.

The general belief was that they were Asian peasants, ignorant of the dangers of boosting to even a modest altitude in a continental winter, or victims of sudden weather changes who had been claimed by frostbite without realising what was happening to them. An hysterical faction, small but vociferous, claimed they were political expendables deliberately cast loose on the geostrophic winds to hinder, even marginally, the flow of western commerce. Hasson had always regarded the latter idea as being unworthy of his consideration, and the fact that it had entered his mind now was yet another pointer to his state of health. He slid his hand into his coat pocket and gripped the container of Serenix capsules, reassuring himself they were available.

In a few minutes the car had reached the airfield and was skirting its perimeter on the way to the flying boat docks. The tall silvery fins of the boats could be seen here and there above the complex of quayside sheds and portable offices. A number of men, their clothing marked with dayglo panels, were flying between the quay and the boats anchored further out in the estuary, registering on the edge of Hasson's vision as a constant agitation of colourful specks.

Nunn brought the car to a halt in a parking bay which was outside the mesh fence of the departure area. As Hasson's department head, he had been burdened with most of the behind-the-scenes work associated with smuggling Hasson out of the country and finding a place where he could live in safe obscurity for three months. No formal machinery existed for hiding and protecting key witnesses whose lives could be under threat, and Captain Nunn had been put to considerable trouble to find a suitable host for Hasson in another country. In the end he had come to an arrangement with a Canadian police officer who had been on an exchange visit to the Coventry force some years earlier. Nunn was a man who hated anything to upset his administrative routine and now he was anxious to get Hasson off his hands.

"We won't go in with you, Rob," he said, switching off the engine. "The less we're seen together the better. No point in taking any chances."

"Chances!" Hasson snorted to show his disapproval of what he thought of as a charade. "What chances? Sullivan is a mobster, but he's also a business man and he knows he'll be finished if he starts killing cops."

Nunn drummed with his fingers on the serrated rim of the steering wheel. "We're not cops Rob—we're *air* cops. And people kill us all the time. How many of your original squad are still alive?"

"Not many." Hasson turned his head away to hide an unexpected, unmanning quiver of his lower lip.

"I'm sorry—I shouldn't have said that." Nunn sounded irritated rather than apologetic.

Colebrook, ever watchful, gripped Hasson's arm just above the elbow and squeezed it firmly. "Take two capsules right now, Rob. That's an order."

Embarrassed and ashamed, Hasson brought the plastic dispenser out of his pocket, fed two green-and-gold capsules into his palm and swallowed them. They felt dry and weightless in his mouth, like the blown-out eggs of tiny birds.

Nunn cleared his throat. "The point I was making is that the Sullivan case is out of the hands of the Air Police and we have to do what SCQ tells us. If they think your evidence is worth the Sullivan organisation's trying to shut you up for good we have to accept what they say. It's their patch."

"I know, but it's all so . . ." Hasson gazed around him helplessly.

"I mean . . . fake identity, fake passport! How am I going to get used to calling myself Haldane?"

"That doesn't seem much of a problem to me," Nunn said brusquely, compressing his lips. "Try to adopt a more positive attitude, Rob. Get yourself off to Canada and do a lot of sleeping and eating and drinking, and enjoy it while you have the chance. We'll send for you when you have to testify."

"Speaking as a medical man, that sounds like good advice." Colebrook opened the door at his side, got out and went to the back of the car. He lifted the lid of the trunk and began unloading Hasson's cases.

"I won't get out," Nunn said, reaching a hand into the rear seat. "Take care of yourself, Rob."

"Thanks." Hasson shook the offered hand and let himself out of the car. The sky had completely cleared now, to the palest wash of blue, and a searching breeze was whipping in from the Atlantic. Hasson shivered as he thought of the thousands of kilometres of open sea that lay between him and his destination. The journey seemed too great for any aircraft, and even more incredible was the idea that only a few months ago he, Robert Hasson, faced with the task of getting to Canada, would have brashly strapped on a counter-gravity harness and made the flight alone, with no protection other than a helmet and heated suit. At the thought of going aloft again, of being able to *fall*, a looseness developed in Hasson's knees and he leaned against the vehicle, taking care to make the action look casual. The enamelled metal chilled his fingers.

"I'll go with you as far as reception," Colebrook said. "Nobody's going to worry about seeing you with a doctor."

"I'd rather go in alone, thanks. I'm all right."

Colebrook smiled approvingly. "That's good. Just remember what the physiotherapist told you about how to lift heavy weights." Hasson nodded, said goodbye to the surgeon and went towards the gate which led to the departure building. He carried a large and a small case in each hand, keeping his back straight and the load in balance. The pain from his spine and the rebuilt joint of his left knee was considerable, but he had learned that movement—no matter how uncomfortable—was his ally. The real pain, the devastating and paralysing agony, came after he was forced to remain immobile for a long period, and then had to perform a once simple action such as getting out of bed. It was as though his body, denying the magic of surgery, had a masochistic yearning for crippledom.

He went into the passenger terminal where he and his baggage were subjected to a series of fairly perfunctory checks. It turned out that there were about twenty other people on his particular flight, which meant that the flying boat had almost its full quota of passengers. For the most part, they were middle-aged couples who had the flustered, expectant look of people who were not used to long-distance travel. Hasson guessed they were going abroad to visit relatives. He stood apart from them, sipping machine-made coffee and wondering why anybody who had the option of remaining safely at home would set out to cross a wintered ocean.

"Your attention, please," called a stewardess who had razor-cut golden hair and neat, hard features. "Flight B0162 is scheduled to take off for St. John's in approximately twenty minutes. Due to the strength and direction of the breeze which has sprung up within the last few hours, we have been forced to anchor the aircraft further out than is usual and our motor launches are having to cope with extra work—but we can avoid delaying our departure if we fly out to the aircraft. Are there any passengers with boarding cards for Flight B0162 who are unable to make a personal flight of half a kilometre?"

Hasson's heart lurched sickeningly as he glanced around the group and saw that all of them were nodding in tentative agreement.

"Very well," the stewardess said, nodding her head. "You will find standard CG harnesses on the rack beside the . . ."

"I'm sorry," Hasson cut in, "I'm not allowed to use a harness."

The girl's eyes flickered briefly and there was a disappointed murmur from the other passengers. Several women glanced at Hasson, their eyes speculative and resentful. He turned away without speaking, feeling the chill air rush upwards past him at terminal velocity as he bombed down into Birmingham's crowded commuter levels after a fall of three thousand metres, and the lights of the city expanded beneath him like a vast jewelled flower . . .

"In that case there's no point in any of us flying." The stewardess's voice was neutral. "If you will all make yourselves comfortable I will call you as soon as a launch is available. We will do everything we can to keep delays to a minimum. Thank you." She went to a communications set in the corner of the glass-walled lounge and began whispering into it.

Hasson set his cup down and, acutely conscious of being stared at, walked into the toilets. He locked himself into a cubicle, leaned against the door for a moment, then took out his medicine dispenser and fed two more capsules into his mouth. The two he had swallowed in the car had not yet taken effect, and as he stood in the sad little closed universe of partitions and tiles, praying for tranquillity, it dawned on him how complete his breakdown had been. He had seen other men crack up under the strain of too much work, too many hours of cross-wind patrols at night when the danger of collision with a rogue flier made the nerves sing like telephone wires in a gale, but always he had viewed the event with a kind of smug incomprehension. Underlying his sympathy and intellectual appreciation of the medical facts had been a faint contempt, a conviction that given his mental stability the wilted air cops, the sick birds, would have been able to shrug off their woes and carry on as before. His sense of security had been so great that he had totally failed to recognise his own warning symptoms—the moods of intense depression, the irritability, the growing pessimism which drained life of its savour. Without realising it, Hasson had been terribly vulnerable, and in that fragile condition—shorn of all his armour—he had gone into the arena against a grinning opponent who wore a black cloak and carried a scythe . . .

A sudden claustrophobia caused Hasson to open the cubicle door. He went to a wash basin, put cold water in it and was splashing some on his face when he became aware of somebody standing beside him. It was one of the passengers from his own flight, a man of about sixty who had a florid complexion and sardonically drooping eyelids.

"Nothing to be ashamed of," the man said in a north country accent.

"What?" Hasson began drying his face.

"Nothing to be ashamed of. That's what I was telling them out there. Some people just can't use a harness, and that's that."

"I suppose you're right." Hasson fought down an urge to tell the stranger he had done a great deal of flying but was temporarily barred from it for medical reasons. If he started justifying himself to every busybody he met he would be doing it for the rest of his life—and there was also the fact that the story was a lie. There was no physical necessity for him to avoid personal flight.

"On the other hand," the red-faced man continued, "some people take to it like a duck takes to water. I was nearly forty when I got my first harness, and within a week I was cloud-running with the best of them."

"Very good," Hasson said, edging away.

"Yes, and I still fly in a tough area. Bradford! The kids up there think nothing of coming in close, deliberate-like, and dropping you twenty or thirty metres." The stranger paused to chuckle. "Doesn't bother me, though. Strong stomach."

"That's great." Hasson hurried to the door, then it occurred to him that a garrulous companion might be just what he needed to numb his mind during the Atlantic crossing. He paused and waited for the other man to catch up with him. "But you're going to Canada the easy way."

"Have to," the man said, tapping himself on the chest. "Lungs won't take the cold any more—otherwise I'd save myself the price of a plane ticket. Bloody robbery, that's what it is."

Hasson nodded agreement as he walked back to the lounge with his new companion. Personal flying was both easy and cheap, and with the advent of the counter-gravity harness conventional aviation had fallen into an abrupt decline. At first it had been simply a matter of economics, then the skies had become too cluttered with people—millions of liberated, mobile, foolhardy, uncontrollable people—for aircraft to operate safely, except in strictly policed corridors. The formerly lucrative passenger traffic across the North Atlantic had been replaced by cargo planes carrying handfuls of passengers on sparse schedules, and the cost per head had risen accordingly.

Rejoining the other passengers, Hasson learned that the older man's name was Dawlish and that he was on the way to Montreal to visit an ailing cousin, possibly in the hope of inheriting some money. Hasson conversed with him for ten minutes, reassured by the sense of calmness that was spreading radially through his system as the Serenix capsules began to do their work. His knowledge that the feeling was artificially induced made it nonetheless precious, and by the time the launch arrived to take the passengers on Flight

B0162 out to their plane he was experiencing a muted euphoria.

He sat near the front during the ride across choppy water to reach the flying boat, feeling a pleasurable excitement at the thought of spending three months abroad. The boat looked prehistoric, with grills over the turbine intakes and armour plating on the airfoil leading edges, but now Hasson had some confidence in the looming machine's ability to take him anywhere in the world. He climbed on board—inhaling the distinctive aroma of engine oil, brine-soaked rope and hot food—and got a window seat near the rear of the passenger compartment. Dawlish sat down opposite him with his back to the movable partition which allowed the cargo space to be expanded or contracted as required.

"Good machines these," Dawlish said, looking knowledgeable. "Based on the Thirties Empire boat design. Very interesting story to them."

As Hasson had half-expected, Dawlish launched into a discourse on the romance of the flying boat, a rambling account which took in its disappearance from world aviation in the Fifties because of the difficulty of pressurising the hull for the high-altitude operation demanded by jet engines, its reappearance in the 21st Century when, of necessity, all aircraft had to fly low and slow.

At another time he might have been bored or irritated, but on this occasion Dawlish was performing a useful function and Hasson concentrated gratefully on the flow of words while the boat's four engines were being started and it was taxied round into the wind. In spite of the capsules he felt a pang of unease as the take-off run seemed to go on for ever, culminating in a thunderous hammering of wave-tops on the underside of the keel, but all at once the noise ceased and the boat was in rock-steady flight. Hasson looked at the solidity of the deck beneath his feet and felt safe.

" . . . monopropellant turbines would work just as well at altitude," Dawlish was saying, "but if you fly low anybody you run into is likely to be reasonably soft and the shielding will stand the impact. Just imagine hitting a frozen body at nearly a thousand kilometres an hour! The Titanic wouldn't be . . ." Dawlish broke off and touched Hasson's knee. "I'm sorry, lad—I shouldn't be talking about that sort of thing."

"I'm all right," Hasson said sleepily, making the belated discovery that for a man in his exhausted state four Serenix capsules had been too much. "You go right ahead. Get it out of your system."

"What do you mean?"

"Nothing." Hasson sincerely wished to be diplomatic, but it had become difficult to perceive shades of meaning in his own words. "You seem to know a lot about flying."

Apparently annoyed at Hasson's tone, Dawlish glanced around him from below sagging eyelids. "Of course, this isn't *real* flying. Cloud-running, that's the thing! You don't know what real flying is until you've strapped on a harness and gone up five hundred, six hundred metres with nothing under your feet but thin air. I only wish I could tell you what it's like."

"That would be . . ." Hasson abandoned the attempt to speak as the conscious world tilted ponderously away from him.

He was three thousand metres above Birmingham, as high as it was possible to go without special heavy-duty suit heaters, at the centre of a sphere of milky radiance created by his flares . . . a short distance away from him the body of his dead partner, Lloyd Inglis, floated upright on height-maintenance power, performing a strange aerial shuffle . . . and, just beyond the range of the flares, Lloyd's murderer was waiting in ambush . . .

There was no human sound as the attack began—only the growing rush of air as the two men's CG harnesses cancelled each other's fields, allowing them to drop like stones . . .

It took a minute for them to fall three thousand metres—a hideous, soul-withering minute in which the howl of the terminal velocity wind was the blast from the chimneys of hell. During that minute the low-level commuter lanes, glowing like a galaxy with the personal lights of tens of thousands of fliers, expanded hungrily beneath him, opening like a carnivorous flower. During that minute, pain and shock robbed him of the powers of thought, and his mind was further obliterated by the obscene grinding of the psychotic killer's body against his own . . .

And then—when it was so late, when it was so desperately late—came the successful disengagement, the breaking free, followed by the futile upward drag of his harness . . . and the impact . . . the ghastly impact with the ground . . . the shattering of bone, and the explosive bursting of spinal disks . . .

Hasson opened his eyes and blinked uncomprehendingly at a

world of sky-bright windows, curved ceiling panels, luggage racks, and the subdued pulsing of aero engines. *I'm in an aircraft,* he thought. *What am I doing in an aircraft?* He sat upright, groggy as a boxer recovering from a knockout blow, and saw that Dawlish had fallen asleep in the seat opposite to him, a micro-reader still clasped in one blue-knuckled hand. The realisation that he had been unconscious for some time was accompanied by a rush of memories, and he rediscovered the fact that he was on his way to Canada, faced with the challenge of a new identity and a new way of life.

The prospect was daunting, but not as daunting as the idea of meeting the challenge in his present condition of drug-fuddled incapacity, held up by a psychotropic crutch. He waited for a few minutes, breathing deeply, then got to his feet and walked to the toilet at the forward end of the passenger compartment. The soundproofing within the toilet was not as good as in the rest of the aircraft, and for a moment he was disconcerted by the pounding of atmospheric fists on the skin of the hull, but he braced himself against the partition and took the medicine dispenser from his pocket. He wrenched the top off it and, without giving himself time for second thoughts, poured a stream of green-and-gold capsules into the toilet bowl.

By the time he got back to his seat he was woozy again, ready to fall asleep, but he had the spare satisfaction that always came from refusing to compromise. He was not the Robert Hasson he used to be, or had imagined himself to be. He felt incomplete, wounded, flawed—but his future was his own personal property, and there was to be no side-stepping of any problems it would bring.

CHAPTER 2

TECHNICAL DIFFICULTIES had closed the transcontinental air corridor west of Regina, so Hasson completed his journey by rail.

It was mid-morning when he reached Edmonton, and on stepping down from the train he was immediately struck by the coldness of the sun-glittering air which washed around him like the waters of a mountain stream. In his previous experience such temperatures allied with brilliant sunshine had only been encountered when patrolling high above the Pennines on a Spring morning. For an instant he was flying again, dangerously poised, with a flight of gulls twinkling like stars far below, and the weakness returned to his knees. He looked around the rail station, anchoring himself to the ground, taking in details of his surroundings. The platform extended a long way beyond the girdered roof, dipping into hard-packed snow which was criss-crossed with tyre tracks. City buildings formed a blocky palisade against the snowfields he could sense to the north. Hasson, wondering how he was going to recognise his escort, examined the people nearest to him. The men seemed huge and dauntingly jovial, many of them dressed in reddish tartan jackets as though conforming to tourists' preconceived notions of how Canadians should look.

Hasson, suddenly feeling overwhelmed and afraid, picked up his cases and moved towards the station exit. As he did so an almost-handsome, olive-skinned man with a pencil-line moustache and exceptionally bright eyes came towards him, hands extended. The stranger's expression of friendliness and pleasure was so intense that Hasson moved out of his way, fearful of perhaps obstructing a family reunion. He glanced back over his shoulder and was surprised to find there was nobody close behind him.

"Rob!" The stranger gripped both of Hasson's shoulders.

"Rob Hasson! It's great to see you again. Really great!"

"I . . ." Hasson gazed into the varnish-coloured eyes which stared back at him with such intemperate affection and was forced to the conclusion that this was his Canadian host, Al Werry. "It's good to see you again."

"Come on, Rob—you look like you could do with a drink." Werry took the cases from Hasson's unresisting fingers and set off with them towards the exit barrier. "I've got a bottle of Scotch in the car outside—and guess what."

"What?"

"It's your favourite. Lockhart's."

Hasson was taken aback. "Thanks, but how did you . . .?"

"That was quite a night we had in that pub—you know the one about ten minutes along the highway from Air Police HQ. What was it called?"

"I can't remember."

"The Haywain," Werry supplied. "You were drinking Lockhart whisky, Lloyd Inglis was on vodka, and I was learning to drink your Boddington's ale. What a night!" Werry reached a sleek-looking car which had a city crest on its side, opened its trunk and began loading the four cases, thus giving Hasson a moment in which to think. He had the vaguest memory of an occasion seven or eight years earlier when he had become involved with providing hospitality for a group of Canadian police officers, but every detail of the evening was lost to him. Now it was obvious that Werry had been one of the visitors and he felt both embarrassed and alarmed by the other man's ability to recall an unimportant event with such clarity.

"Hop in there, Rob, and we'll shake this place—I want to get you to Tripletree in time for lunch. May is cooking up moose steaks for us, and I'll bet you never tasted moose." While he was speaking Werry slipped out of his overcoat, folded it carefully and placed it on the car's rear seat. His chocolate-brown uniform, which carried the insignia of a city reeve, was crisply immaculate and when he sat down he spent some time smoothing the cloth of the tunic behind him to prevent it being wrinkled by the driving seat. Hasson opened the passenger door and got in, taking equal care to ensure that his spine was straight and well supported in the lumbar region.

"Here's what you need," Werry said, taking a flat bottle from a dash compartment and handing it to Hasson. He smiled indulgently, showing square healthy teeth.

"Thanks." Hasson dutifully accepted the bottle and took a swig from it, noticing as he tilted his head that there was a police-style counter-gravity harness flying suit lying on the rear seat beside Werry's coat. The neat spirit tasted warmish, flat and unnaturally strong, but he pretended to savour it, a task which became Herculean when it seared into one of the mouth ulcers which had been troubling him for weeks.

"You hold on to that—it's more'n an hour's run to Tripletree." Werry spun up the car's turbine as he spoke and a few seconds later they were surging into a northbound traffic stream. As the car emerged from among the downtown buildings expanses of blue sky became visible and Hasson saw above him a fantastic complex of aerial highways. The bilaser images looked real but not real—curves, ramps, straights, trumpet-shaped entrances and exits, all apparently carved from coloured gelatine and bannered across the sky to guide and control the flux of individual fliers whose business brought them into the city. Thousands of dark specks moved along the insubstantial ducts, like the representation of a gas flow in a physics text.

"Pretty, isn't it? Some system!" Werry leaned forward, peering upwards with enthusiasm.

"Very nice." Hasson tried to find a comfortable posture in the car's too-pliant upholstery as he studied the three-dimensional pastel-coloured projections. Similar traffic control techniques had been tried in Britain back in the days when there still had been hope of reserving some territory for conventional aircraft, but they had been abandoned as too costly and too complicated. With millions of individuals airborne above a small island, many of them highly resistant to discipline, it had been found most expedient to go for a simple arrangement of columnar route markers with bands of colour at different altitudes. The most basic bilaser installations could cope with the task of projecting the solid-seeming columns, and they had a further advantage in that they left the aerial environment looking comparatively uncluttered. To Hasson's eyes, the confection hovering above Edmonton resembled the entrails of some vast semi-transparent mollusc.

"You feeling all right, Rob?" Werry said. "Is there anything I can do for you?"

Hasson shook his head. "I've been travelling too long, that's all."

"They told me you got yourself all smashed up."

"Just a broken skeleton," Hasson said, modifying an old joke. "How much did they tell you, anyway?"

"Not much. It's better that way, I guess. I'm telling everybody you're my cousin from England, that your name's Robert Haldane, that you're an insurance salesman and you're convalescing from a bad car smash."

"It sounds plausible enough."

"I hope so." Werry drummed his fingers on the steering wheel, signalling his dissatisfaction. "It's a funny sort of set-up, though. With England having separate air police, I mean. I never thought you'd get mixed up with big-time organised crime."

"It was just the way things worked out. Lloyd Inglis and I were busting a gang of young angels, and when Lloyd got killed the . . ." Hasson broke off as the car swerved slightly. "I'm sorry. Didn't they say?"

"I didn't know Lloyd was dead."

"I can't take it in myself yet." Hasson stared at the road ahead, which was like a black canal banked with snow. "One of the gang was the son of a mob chief who was buying up respectability as if it was development land, and the boy was carrying papers which were going to wipe out his old man's investment. It's a long story, and complicated . . ." Hasson, tired of talking, hoped he had said enough to satisfy Werry's professional curiosity.

"Okay, let's forget all that sort of stuff, *cousin*." Werry smiled and gave Hasson an exaggerated wink. "All I want is for you to relax and get yourself built up again. You're goin' to have the time of your life in the next three months. Believe me."

"I do." Hasson glanced discreetly, gratefully, at his new companion. Werry's body was hard and flat, with a buoyant curvature to the muscles which suggested a natural strength carefully maintained by exercise. He seemed to take an ingenuous pleasure in the perfection of his uniform, something which combined with his Latin-American looks to give him the aura of a swaggering young colonel in a revolutionary republic. Even his handling of the car—slightly aggressive, slightly flamboyant—spoke of a man who was perfectly at home in his environment, taking up its challenges with a zestful confidence. Hasson, envious of the other man's intact and gleaming psychological armour, wondered how it had been possible for him to forget his first meeting with Werry.

"By the way," Werry said, "I didn't tell the folks at home—that's May and Ginny, and my boy Theo—anything about you. Anything apart from the official story, that is. Thought it better just to keep things to ourselves. It's simpler that way."

"You're probably right." Hasson mulled over the new information for a moment. "Didn't your wife think it was a bit odd when you produced a brand-new cousin out of thin air?"

"May isn't my wife—not yet anyway. Sybil left me about a year ago, May and her mother only moved in last month, so it's all right—I could have cousins all over the world, for all they know."

"I see." Hason felt a throb of unease at the prospect of having to meet and co-habit with three more strangers, and it came to him once again that he had joined the ranks of life's walking wounded. The car was now speeding along a straight highway which cut through immensities of sun-blinding snow. He fumbled in his breast pocket, produced a pair of darkened glasses and put them on, glad of the barrier they set up against the pressures of an unmanageable universe. He shifted to an easier position in his seat, cradling the unwanted bottle of whisky, and tried to come to terms with the new Robert Hasson.

The deceptively commonplace term "nervous breakdown", he had discovered, was a catch-all for a host of devastating mental and physical symptoms—but the knowledge that he was suffering from a classical and curable illness did nothing to alleviate those symptoms. No matter how often he told himself he would be back to normal in the not-too-distant future, his depressions and fears remained implacable enemies, swift to strike, tenacious, slow to relinquish their grip. In his own case, he appeared to have regressed emotionally to relive the turmoils of adolescence.

His father, Desmond Hasson, had been a West Country village storekeeper driven by circumstance to work in the city, and had never even begun to adapt to his new surroundings. Naïve, awkward, pathologically shy, he had lived out the life of a hopeless exile a mere two hundred kilometres from his birthplace, bound by the rigidity of his outlook, always whispering when in public lest the difference in his accent should draw curious glances. His marriage to a tough-minded city girl had served only to let the incomprehensible strangeness of the world of factories and office blocks invade his home, and he had become perpetually reserved and uncommunicative. It had come as a bitter disappointment to him to find that his son responded naturally and easily to an urban environment, and for some years he had done his best to correct what he regarded as a serious character defect. There had been the long, uninformative walks in the country (Desmond Hasson knew surprisingly little about the world of nature he espoused); the futile hours of fishing in polluted streams; the boredom of enforced labour in a vegetable garden. Young Rob Hasson had disliked all of those things, but the real psychological marks had been caused by his father's attempts to mould his essential nature.

He had been a gregarious boy, not averse to speaking his mind, and the worst personality conflicts had arisen from this fact. Time after time he had been quelled, humbled, desolated by the admonition—always delivered in a shocked and betrayed undertone—that a proposed course of action would cause people to *look* at him. He had grown up with the implanted conviction that the most scandalous thing he could ever do would be to draw the attention of others in public. There had been other strictures, notably those concerned with sex, but the principal one, the one which clung longest and made life most difficult, had been that concerning the need for self-effacement. Even as a young adult, at college and during a brief spell in the army, each time he had been called upon to get up on his feet and address any kind of assembly he had been plagued and undermined by visions of panic-stricken blue eyes and by the parental voice whispering, "Everybody will *look* at you!"

Hasson had eventually broken the conditioning, and—with his father long dead—had thought himself free of it for ever, but the impact of nervous illness appeared to have shattered his adult character like a glass figurine. It was as if his father had begun to achieve a posthumous victory, recreating himself in his only son. He found it intensely difficult to sustain any kind of a conversation, and the thought of having to enter a house of strangers filled him with a cool dread. Hasson stared sombrely at the unfolding alien snowscapes and yearned desperately to be back in his two-roomed flat in Warwick, with the door locked and the undemanding companionship of a television set for solace.

Al Werry, as though sensing his need, remained silent in the following hour except for the passing on of scraps of information about local geography. In between times, the police radio made occasional popping and growling noises, but no calls came through on it. Hasson took the opportunity to recharge his spiritual batteries and was feeling slightly more competent when a tangle of pale-glowing aerial sculptures appeared above the horizon, letting him know they were drawing close to Tripletree. He was taking in the broad outlines of the traffic control system when his eye was caught by the silhouette of a peculiar structure close to the city, stark against the background of luminous pastels. From the distance it resembled a monstrous, single-stemmed flower, grown to a height of perhaps four hundred metres. He speculated briefly about its purpose, then turned to Werry.

"What's that thing?" he said. "It can't be a water tower, or can it?"

"There's nothing wrong with your eyes, Rob." Werry spent a few seconds staring straight ahead, satisfying himself that he too could see the object clearly. "That's our local landmark, Morlacher's Folly—otherwise known as the Chinook Hotel."

"Strange architecture for a hotel."

"Yeah, but not as strange as you would think. You know what a chinook is?"

"A warm breeze you get in the wintertime."

"That's right, except that we don't always get it. Around here it has a habit of streaming over us at a height of a hundred or two hundred metres. Sometimes as low as fifty. It can be ten below zero at ground level, so we're going around freezing, and up there the birds are sunbathing at ten and fifteen degrees above. That's what was in old Harry Morlacher's mind when he built the hotel—the residential part is right up there in the warm air stream. It was meant to be a high-priced R&R spot for oil execs from all over Athabasca."

"Something went wrong?"

"*Everything* went wrong." Werry gave a quiet snort, a sound which might have been indicative of appreciation, awe or contempt. "None of the construction outfits around here had ever tried building a giant lollipop before, so the costs kept going up and up till Morlacher was down to near his last cent. Then they developed new ways of scooping up the tar sands and cleaned out what was left of the easy stuff in a couple of years. Then monopropellant engines came in and nobody had much use for our oil anymore, so the Chinook Hotel never took in a paying customer. Not one! Talk about a fool and his money!"

Hasson, who had little expertise with money, clicked his tongue. "Anybody can make a mistake."

"Not that sort of mistake. It takes a special talent to make that sort of mistake." Werry grinned at Hasson and adjusted the angle of his cap, looking scornful, tough, healthy and well-adjusted, the picture of an up-and-coming career cop, a man with complete confidence in his own abilities. Hasson felt a fresh pang of envy.

"Still, it makes a good talking point," he said.

Werry nodded. "We'll be going right by it on the way into town. We can stop there and you can have a close look."

"I'd like that."

There was little else of interest in the flat white landscape and Hasson kept his gaze fixed on the remarkable structure as it steadily expanded in the frame of the car's windshield. It was only when they had approached to within a kilometre that he began to appreciate the full daring of the unconventional architecture. The central column looked impossibly slim as it soared skywards to blossom outwards into an array of radial beams supporting the circular mass of the hotel proper. It gave the appearance of having been forged from a single piece of stainless steel, although he was sure that seams would become visible upon close inspection. Sunlight glinted on the glass-and-plastics exterior of the hotel section, making it look remote and unattainable, an Olympian resort for a godlike breed of men.

"There isn't much room inside that stem for a lift . . . elevator," Hasson commented as the car reached the outskirts of Tripletree and began to pass widely separated high-income dwellings perched on snow-covered hummocks.

"No room," Werry said. "The plan was for two tubular scenic elevators running up beside the pylon, but things never got that far. You can see the holes for them on the underside of the hotel."

Hasson, narrowing his eyes against the intense light from the sky, had just managed to pick out two circular apertures when his attention was caught by a moving speck in the upper air close to the hotel. "There's a flier up there."

"Is there?" Werry sounded uninterested. "Could be Buck Morlacher—old Harry's son. Buck or one of his men."

"The place isn't in use, is it?"

"It's in use, all right—but not the way the Morlachers had in mind," Werry said grimly. "We've got angels here too, you know, and the Chinook makes a dandy roost for them. At night they come in from all over the province for their get-togethers."

Hasson visualised the task of trying to police the huge eyrie at night and there was an icy heaving in his stomach. "Can't you seal the place up?"

"Too much glass. They can pick a window anywhere and cut through the bars and they're in."

"What about CG field neutralisers? A building like that must have had them to keep off peepers."

"The money ran out before they were installed." Werry glanced at his wristwatch. "Look, Rob, you must be real hungry by this time. I'll take you right on home now to eat and we can stop by for a look at the hotel some other time. How does that sound to you?"

Hasson was on the point of falling in with the suggestion out of courtesy when he realised he had no desire for food. Furthermore, making a closer inspection of the fantastic building would stave off the ordeal of having to meet the other members of Werry's household.

"I couldn't look at food just yet," he said, testing the position. "A column that height must have one hell of a foundation."

"Yeah—in the ground, where you can't see it."

"All the same . . ."

"Tourists," Werry sighed, swinging the car to the left to pick up a tree-lined avenue which ran towards the hotel. At this proximity, for the occupants of a vehicle, the building registered on the vision as nothing but a silvery mast sprouting from behind ordinary buildings and making a dizzy ascent to unseen regions. The idea of following that slim pylon upwards for four hundred metres and finding a world of conference halls, ballrooms, cocktail bars and bedrooms seemed utterly preposterous, as much a part of a fairy tale as a giant's castle at the top of a beanstalk.

Hasson looked about him with interest as the car reached a flat and undeveloped tract of land which would have formed spacious grounds for the hotel. Its boundary was marked by a four-strand wire fence which had been knocked down in several places, and here and there beneath the snow it was possible to pick out old scars made by earth-moving equipment. The air of desolation, of a battle that had been lost, was added to by the state of the low circular building which surrounded the base of the support column. Most of its windows had star-shaped holes and the walls were colourful samplers of aerosol graffiti. A strip of waterproof skin that had almost been detached from the roof stirred gently in the breeze.

As the car came to a halt Hasson noticed another vehicle—an expensive-looking, wine-coloured sports model—parked just inside the line of the fence. A fur-hatted man in his thirties was leaning against it with a shotgun cradled in his arms. He was wearing a one-piece flying suit, the glistening black material of which was crossed by the fluorescent orange straps of a CG harness. Hearing the other car arrive, he turned his head towards Werry and Hasson for a moment—flashing sunlight from mirrored lenses—then resumed his concentrated study of the lofty upper section of the hotel.

"That's Buck Morlacher," Werry said. "Guarding the family investment."

"Really? With a gun?"

"That's just for show, mainly. Buck likes to think he's a frontiersman."

Hasson paused in the act of opening the car door. "He isn't wearing panniers. Don't tell me he flies with a shotgun just held in his hands."

"No chance!" Werry tugged the peak of his cap down a little. "It wouldn't matter much, anyway. There's nobody around here for it to fall on."

"Yes, but . . ." Hasson stopped speaking as he realised he was on the verge of interfering in things which were not his concern. One of the most universal and necessary legislations relating to personal flight was the one which forbade the transportation of dense objects, except in specially approved pannier bags. Even with that precaution the annual death toll from falling objects was unacceptably high, and there was no country in the world where the breaking of that particular law did not bring severe mandatory penalties. All Hasson's instincts told him Morlacher had just flown with the gun, or was about to fly, and he felt a profound relief over the fact that the law enforcement task was not his. It was work for a fit, hard man in full possession of himself.

"Are you getting out?" Werry said, again glancing at his watch.

"Can't see anything from in here." Hasson pushed open the passenger door, swung his feet sideways and froze as his back locked itself into immobility with a sensation like bone grinding on dry bone. He caught his breath and began trying different grips on the doorframe as he struggled with the engineering problem of how to hoist his skeleton into an upright position. Werry got out at the other side without noticing, adjusted his cap, checked to see how his gleaming boots were faring on the snow, tugged his tunic straight at the back, and approached Morlacher with careful tread.

"Mornin', Buck," he said. "Going to do a little duck shooting?"

"Go away, Al—I'm busy." Morlacher continued staring upwards, his eyes hidden behind chips of pale blue sky. He was a large, overweight man with copper-coloured hair and a triangular patch of bright pink on each cheek. His lips were drawn back, exposing teeth which seemed to be inhumanly thick and strong, with heavy molars in place of incisors. Hasson immediately felt afraid of him.

"I can see you're busy," Werry said pleasantly. "Just wondered what you're busy *at*."

"What's the matter with you?" A look of impatience appeared on Morlacher's face as he lowered his head to stare at Werry. "You know I'm doing the work you should be doing—if you'd any balls. Why don't you just get back into your kiddycar and leave me to it? All right?"

Werry glanced back at Hasson, who had managed to draw himself into a standing position with his arms along the top of the car door. "Now you listen to me, Buck," Werry said. "What makes you . . .?"

"They were up there last night again," Morlacher cut in. "Having one of their dirty parties—violating my property—*violating* it, do you hear? And what do you do about it? Nothing. That's what you do—*nothing!*" Morlacher scowled, pulling his colourless eyebrows together, and directed his mirrored gaze towards Hasson as though becoming aware of him for the first time. Hasson, still trying to establish whether or not he could stand up unsupported, looked away into the distance. He detected a movement at the upper edge of his vision and raised his eyes to see a flier swooping down from the hotel.

"There might be one or two of them still holed out up there," Morlacher went on, "and if that's so, Starr and I are going to flush them out and deal with them ourselves. The old way."

"There's no need for that sort of talk," Werry protested. He was staring, perplexed, at Morlacher when the descending flier closed in on him from above and behind. He was a wispy-bearded youngster, wearing a blue flying suit and carrying a pump-action shotgun slung across his back. As Hasson watched, he moved a hand to his belt and deliberately switched off his counter-gravity field while still three metres in the air. He dropped instantaneously, but the momentum remaining from his curving descent brought him into a thudding collision with Werry's shoulder. Werry sprawled on the ground, his face driven into the snow.

"Sorry, Al. Sorry. Sorry." The young man helped Werry to his feet and began brushing snow from his uniform. "It was a pure accident—the glare from the snow blinded me." He was winking at Morlacher as he spoke.

Hasson felt a rush of adrenalin through his system as he looked at Al Werry, waiting for him to take the action the situation cried out for. Werry straightened up and looked uncertainly down at the newcomer who was stooped before him brushing his clothes with exaggerated gestures of concern. *Now,* Hasson willed. *Now, before any more time passes. Now, while he's set up for you in all his arrogance.*

Werry shook his head and—disastrously—began to smile. "Know something, Starr Pridgeon? I don't think you're *ever* going to get the hang of that harness."

"Know something, Al? I think you're right." The youngster gave a bray of laughter and in the middle of it, just as Morlacher had done, turned and fixed his gaze on Hasson as though seeing him for the first time. Hasson, veteran of a thousand such encounters, recognised the imitative borrowing of a mannerism and guessed at once that Morlacher was the dominant partner of the pair. He remained leaning on the car door, tentatively trying to straighten his back as Pridgeon came towards him. Pain flared in his joints. They were machine bearings which had been sabotaged with carborundum powder, robbing him of mobility.

"This must be Al's cousin from England," Pridgeon said. "What do you think of Canada, Al's cousin?"

"I haven't had time to form an opinion," Hasson said steadily.

Pridgeon glanced at the others. "Don't he talk nice?" He turned back to Hasson. "Wasn't that accident the dumbest thing you ever saw?"

"I didn't really see it."

"No?" Pridgeon examined him critically for a moment. "You a cripple or something?"

To his horror, Hasson found his lips arranging themselves in the shape of a smile. "Almost."

"Huh!" Pridgeon walked away looking dissatisfied and stood beside Morlacher, and Hasson realised the older man had summoned him with a slight inclination of his head. His guess about the relationship was confirmed, but the insight was worthless.

"Did you see anything up there?" Morlacher said to Pridgeon, as though they were alone together and nothing had happened.

"Nope. Anybody's up there, they're keeping away from the windows."

"I'll go up with you." Morlacher began tightening the straps of his harness.

"Just so long as you don't carry that shotgun with you," Werry said severely. "We can't have you just blasting off at people."

Morlacher continued addressing Pridgeon. "I'll take this shotgun up with me, and if I see anybody I'll blast off at them."

"Well, I don't know how you characters feel, but I'm hungry," Werry said, suddenly breezy and jovial as he turned to Hasson. "Come on, Rob—May's going to get mad at us if we don't show up in time for those steaks."

He walked to his car and dropped into the driving seat, causing the vehicle to rock on its suspension. Hasson, who had just established that it was now safe for him to move, lowered himself back into the car and closed the door. He placed his hands on his knees and gazed fixedly at them while Werry started the car, drove it in a semicircle across the uneven snow and took them back out to the road. A minute of silence was all he could endure.

"Al," he said quietly, "are you going to put in a call?"

"A call?" Werry sounded genuinely surprised. "What for?"

"You *saw* Pridgeon commit a TDO—he was carrying a shotgun on an ordinary shoulder sling. And Morlacher's going to do it, too."

"I wouldn't worry about that too much. Besides, it was on Buck's private property."

"Which doesn't count in air law."

Werry laughed. "Relax, Rob. This isn't the old country. People aren't shoulder-to-shoulder on the ground here. We've got millions of square kilometres of open land you could drop whole city blocks on without anybody paying any heed."

"But . . ." Hasson tightened his grip on his knees, and the knuckles shone through the skin like ivory hillocks, each bifurcated by a thin pink line. He had realised why he could not remember his first meeting with Werry—the man he had believed Werry to be simply did not exist.

"Pridgeon knocked you down on purpose, you know," he said, reminding himself it was none of his business, but unable to keep the words in check.

"He's always horsing around like that," Werry replied carelessly. "High spirits. It doesn't mean a thing."

That's where you're wrong, Hasson thought. *The symbolism meant everything.* "From what I saw . . ."

"I thought you didn't see anything," Werry cut in. "When Starr asked you, you said you hadn't seen anything."

"Yes, but . . ." Hasson was stung by Werry's remark, mainly because there was no denying it, and he lapsed into a shamed, recriminatory silence. The car reached the business section of Tripletree and he began to study the unfamiliar design of the various stores and office buildings, retreating inwards, picking out unfamiliar elements, noting the different ways in which it was possible to combine windows, walls and doors, and nostalgically comparing what he saw to the homely architecture of English rural villages. The pavements were crowded with lunchtime shoppers, many of whom wore brightly coloured flying suits as protection against the cold. Two policemen—one of them fat and middle-aged, the other looking barely pubescent—nodded amiably at Werry as the car paused at an intersection. He gave them a parody of an official salute, then nodded and grinned, secure and comfortable again in his role, as the fat man wielded an imaginary knife and fork. Both policemen turned immediately and hurried into a hamburger bar.

"Always eating, those two," Werry commented. "Still, it means I generally know where to find them."

Hasson, surprised at the degree of informality in Werry's relationship with his men, seized on it as yet another indicator that he was alone, adrift, orphaned in an alien world. He was sinking luxuriously to new depths of gloom when he became aware that the car was again entering a residential area after having traversed only three or four downtown streets.

"How many people live in Tripletree?" he said, looking about him in some surprise.

"Twenty-six thousand at the last count." Werry gave him a humorous glance. "We still call it a city, though. When the provinces all became autonomous and got their own governments they wanted to be as much like real honest-to-God countries as they could, so they didn't issue charters for anything but cities. There aren't any villages or towns in Alberta. Just cities. Hundreds of them." He laughed and flicked up the peak of his cap, his bonhomie apparently fully restored.

"I see." Hasson tried to digest the information. "And how many men in your department?"

"Actually on the street—four. That was half of my force you saw disappearing into Ronnie's diner. The other half handles air traffic."

"It doesn't seem enough men."

"I manage—and the job carries the official rank of reeve. If I transfer to a big city it'll be as reeve."

Hasson tried to visualise ways of running an effective police force with only four men, but his imagination balked at the task. He was on the point of asking further questions when Werry slowed the car down and turned into a short avenue of white-painted frame houses. The snow had not been cleared from it, as in the main thoroughfare, and it lined the street in fudge-coloured ridges. Hasson's heart began to pound as he realised they had reached

Werry's home and he was close to the meeting with his family. The car crunched to a halt about halfway along the avenue, outside a house which was partly hidden by several young fir trees.

"This is it," Werry said cheerfully. "Rob, you'll have your feet under the table in no time."

Hasson tried to smile. *Just remember,* Dr. Colebrook had told him once, *a person who has had a nervous breakdown and dealt with it successfully is far better equipped to face life than somebody who has never been through the experience. The battle for self-control reveals inner strengths and reserves which otherwise would never have been discovered.* Remembering the words, Hasson tried to draw comfort from them as, fearful of looking at the house in case he encountered strangers' eyes, he opened the car door and lowered his feet to the ground. He discovered that getting out a few minutes earlier at the hotel had helped to free his spine and lumbar muscles, and that he was able to stand up quite normally. Grateful for the respite, he insisted on taking two of his cases out of Werry's hands and carrying them up the path to the house.

Werry opened the outer and inner front doors with a flourish and ushered him into an atmosphere which smelt warmly of cooking, wax polish and camphor. A staircase ran up from the right side of the smallish hall, whose space was further encroached upon by an old-fashioned coatstand which was bulging with a variety of heavy garments, quilted flying suits and CG harnesses. Framed photographs and some highly amateurish watercolours hung on the walls, creating an air of domesticity which made Hasson feel more of an exile than ever because the home to which they belonged was not his home.

He was looking around him, smothered and trapped, when a door at the end of the hall was opened by a woman of about thirty. She was of medium height and fair-haired, with a lean-hipped yet busty figure, and the exact kind of full-lipped, sulky good looks that Hasson had seen in a hundred old flat-screen movies in cinema clubs. This he thought, was the saloon girl who enjoyed her work, the gangster's girl friend, the chick on the back of the big bike, the roadside café waitress for whose favours truck drivers beat each other down with chair legs. She was dressed for the multiple part, in high-heeled shoes, toreador pants and a white T-shirt. Hasson was unable to meet her gaze.

"May," Werry said, his voice filled with omnidirectional pride, "I'd like you to meet my cousin, Rob Haldane. He's been travelling for days and he's hungry. Isn't that right, Rob?"

"That's right," Hasson agreed, accepting that there was no diplomatic way of making Werry see that his principal requirement was for solitude and rest. "How do you do?"

"Hello, Rob." May took his extended hand, and on the instant of contact gave him a sudden smile, coy and direct at the same time, as though some unexpected human chemistry had been worked, taking her by surprise. The trick was so unsubtle that it embarrassed Hasson, and yet he immediately felt flattered.

Werry beamed at them both. "We ought to have a drink. What did you do with the bottle, Rob?"

"Here." Hasson discovered he had slipped the bottle of whisky into his topcoat pocket. He was in the act of producing it when they were joined in the hall by a sharp-featured, thin-shouldered woman of about sixty. She was modishly dressed as though about to set off for a party, with an abundance of jewellery and hair tinted to match her coppertex suit.

"And this is Ginny Carpenter—May's mother," Werry said. "Ginny, meet Rob."

"Pleased." She looked up at Hasson through narrowed eyes and made no move to shake hands. "You're the one who nearly killed hisself in a car."

Hasson was taken aback. "That's right."

"Haven't they got any good hospitals back in England?"

"Now, Ginny," Werry put in placatingly. "Rob's had all the hospital treatment he needs. He's here to rest and build himself up."

"He needs it," Ginny said, still examining Hasson critically. "Have to see what a couple of months of good food will do for him."

Hasson tried to think of a swift retort which would let the woman know he had been accustomed to eating well all his life and expected to continue doing so when he left Canada, but the abrasiveness of her manner had thrown his thoughts into disarray. He stared down at her, dumb and helpless, as he strove to find the right words.

"Were you about to have a belt?" she said, forestalling him, glancing significantly at the bottle in his hand. "If you need it, go right ahead and have it—the smell doesn't bother me."

The phrases which Hasson so desperately needed to put together collided with those which were already swirling in his mind, rendering him even more incapable of speech than before. He turned to the others in the little group. Werry was nodding eagerly, expectantly, as though enjoying a bantering contest between life-long friends; May was still regarding him with wide-eyed, misty candour, projecting waves of startled tenderness. Hasson suppressed an urge to flee.

"That's my bottle, Ginny," Werry said, after what seemed a long time. "Rob brought it in from the car for me."

"Why didn't he say so?" Ginny snapped as she went back into the room from which she had emerged. "I'm going to put the steaks under the grill. Come on, girl! You're not very ambitious today, and there's a load of extra work to do." May obediently followed after her, giving Hasson a last liquid look as she closed the door.

"That Ginny's a real character," Werry said, chuckling. "Always the same—doesn't care what she says to *anybody.* You should have seen your face when she made the crack about bending your elbow!"

Hasson smiled in return, strickenly, wondering how insensitive it was possible for a man to be. "I'm a bit tired. If you don't mind, I'd like to go up to my room."

"You've hardly touched this," Werry said disappointedly, holding the whisky bottle up to the light. "I got it specially for you."

"Thanks, but I'm . . . Is my room upstairs?"

"Follow me." Werry picked up the larger pair of cases and led the way up the narrow stair. He installed Hasson in a pleasant square room which had a double bed and framed photographs of ice hockey teams on the walls. The furnishings were modern except for one glass-fronted bookcase filled with dark cloth-bound volumes whose titles had been eroded to isolated specks of gold or silver. There were two windows admitting a white light whose main direction was upwards, reflected from the snow outside, creating an airy ambience similar to that of the passenger cabin of the flying boat in which he had crossed the Atlantic. Hasson surveyed the room, seeing it with a preternatural clarity which came from the knowledge that it was to be his private fortress for months to come. He checked that there was a lock on the door and almost at once picked out the best place to set up a portable television.

"Bathroom and toilet are just along the landing," Werry said helpfully. "As soon as you get yourself sorted out come down to lunch. Theo is getting out of school early today, and he'll want to meet you too."

"I'll be right down," Hasson replied, willing the other man to leave. As soon as he was alone he lay down on the bed, coaxing his body into relaxation, staring at the shifting twig patterns on the ceiling. *Where are they*? he thought. *Where are the inner strengths and reserves that Dr. Colebrook promised me*? He pressed the back of a hand to his lips and closed his eyes to shut out the merciless white radiance which surrounded him like a besieging army on all sides.

CHAPTER 3

HIS FIRST MEAL in the Werry domicile was even more of an ordeal than Hasson had anticipated. Four places had been set at a circular table in the kitchen, Hasson's distinguished from the others by the presence of a brimming tumbler of neat whisky which produced a queasy feeling in his stomach each time he looked at it. He sat down with Werry and May Carpenter while her mother, with a black cigarette clinging to her upper lip, orchestrated the meal from a standing position at the cooker. She filled each plate in person from various pans, like an army cook, paying scant heed to stated preferences. Hasson, who liked his steak well done, was given a wedge-shaped slab which had been seared black on the outside but was oozing pinkly from several fissures.

"No sauce for me," he said as Ginny reached for an outsized ladle.

"Needs sauce," she replied, dousing everything on his plate with a silty fluid and placing it before him. Hasson glanced at Werry, hoping he would fulfil his obligations as host and come to the rescue, but Werry was busy grimacing happily at May and trying to snatch a ribbon from her hair. He was still wearing his full uniform except for the cap, and looked like a garrison soldier flirting with a new girl. May responded by frowning at him, tossing her head and continually smoothing her hair down with both hands, an action which might have been designed to show off the voluptuousness of her breasts. Hasson was fascinated against his will, and kept being discomfited by the discovery that at the moment of maximum uplift May's gaze was always fixed innocently on his face. In desperation, while waiting for Ginny to sit down, he distracted himself with the whisky, taking minute sips which were barely enough to wet his lips. The months ahead suddenly seemed unbearable, an endurance test he was bound to fail unless his defences were shored up without delay.

"Al," he said, keeping his voice casual, "are there any shops, stores, nearby where I could buy or rent a portable television set?"

Werry raised his eyebrows. "There's a nutty idea for you! We've got a new solid-image job right there in the front room. Two-metre stage. May and Ginny are always watching it, and you can sit with them any time you want. Isn't that right, May?"

May nodded. "The Nabisco Night Club is on tonight."

Hasson tried to smile, unable to reveal that he planned to lock himself in his room and turn it into an outpost of his homeland by taking nothing but British shows from the satellite system. "Ah . . . I'm a pretty poor sleeper these days. These nights, I should say. I need a set in my bedroom for when I can't sleep."

"Other people need to sleep," Ginny Carpenter put in as she joined them at the table with a loaded plate.

"I'd be using the ear pieces. There'd be no . . ."

"Seems a waste of money when there's a new solid-image set with a two-metre stage right there in the front room," Werry said carelessly. "I'll tell you what I'll do, though—I'll take you into town with me on Tuesday morning and introduce you to my buddy, Bill Ratzin. He'll fix you up at the right price."

Hasson did a mental calculation and decided he could not wait four days. "Thanks, but if you don't mind I'd like to . . ."

"Good food going to waste here," Ginny reprimanded.

Hasson lowered his head and began to eat. The moose steak was more edible than he had feared, but the flavour which got through the coating of sauce reminded him strongly of rabbit and after a few small mouthfuls he was unable to continue with it. He began marking time by eating thin slices of carrot which had been liberally glazed with brown sugar and which to him tasted like sweets. Werry was the first to notice his lack of appetite and began to chivvy him loudly, only subsiding when Ginny explained that people who were accustomed to a low standard of living were often unable to cope with rich food. Hasson managed to think of several apt replies, but each time he considered putting them into words he saw his father's panic-stricken blue eyes and heard the well-remembered voice saying, "Everybody will *look* at you." May Carpenter kept giving him sympathetic smiles and making overtly tactful efforts to discuss his journey, but only succeeded in making him feel more gauche and inept than before. He devoted all his mind to ensuring that no particle of food found its way into one of the painful mouth ulcers, and prayed for the meal to come to an end.

"Great stuff," Werry announced as soon as he had finished his coffee. "I'm going into the office for an hour—just to make sure I've still got an office—then I'll pick Theo up coming out of school and run him home."

Seizing his chance, Hasson followed Werry out to the hall. "Listen, Al, I might as well admit it—I've turned into a real TV fanatic since they brought in these solid-image jobs. Can I ride into town with you and pick myself up a set this afternoon?"

"If that's what you want to do." Werry looked puzzled. "Get your coat."

When he got outside Hasson saw at once that the weather had changed. A shutter of low cloud had been drawn across the sky and the air had a chill metallic smell which promised more snow. Against the leaden backdrop, the light-sculpted aerial highways of the city's traffic control system glowed vividly and were as solid looking as neon tubes. The gloominess of the overcast reminded Hasson of winter afternoons in Britain and had the effect of improving his spirits a little. In a grey world his bedroom would be a cocoon of safety and warmth, with its door locked and the curtains drawn, and a television set and a bottle to keep him company and absolve him from any need to think or live a life of his own.

On the way into town he gazed about him with something approaching contentment, picking out one Christmas card scene after another. The car was cruising on the main road into town when the radio hissed loudly and a call came through.

"Al, this is Henry Corzyn," a man's voice said. "I know you didn't want any calls this afternoon, with your cousin being here and all that, but we've got a serious AC here and I think you'd better come over."

"An aerial collision?" Werry sounded interested, but not particularly worried. "Somebody taking a short cut? Flying outside the beams?"

"No. Some kids were bombing the east approach, and one of them misjudged it and hit some guy square on. They might both be dead. You'd better get over here, Al."

Werry swore fervently as he took directions from the policeman and slewed the car into a street leading east. He switched on emergency lights and a siren, and the already sparse surface traffic melted away into the greyness before him.

"Sorry about this, Rob," he said. "I'll get it over with as quickly as I can."

"It's all right," Hasson said, his feeling of insularity shattered. He had seen the results of bombing accidents many times during his career and knew the sort of situation into which Werry was now being precipitated. With the advent of the automobile, man had been transformed into the swiftest creature on the face of the earth, given a new dimension of freedom. That freedom had been too much for many people to handle, and the outcome had been a death toll in the same grisly league as those produced by more ancient scourges such as war, famine and disease. Then man had learned to put a judo hold on gravity, turning its strength back on itself, and had become the swiftest creature in the air, and with his new freedom—to soar with the lark and outstrip the eagle, to straddle the rainbow and follow the sunset around the red rim of the world—the Fifth Horseman, the one who rode a winged steed, had come fully into being.

The youngster who might once have killed himself and some of his fellows with the aid of a motor cycle or fast car now had a new repertoire of dangerous stunts, all of them designed to prove he was immortal—all of them frequently demonstrating the opposite. A favourite game was aerial chicken, in which two fliers would grapple high in the air and fall like stones as their CG fields cancelled each other out. The first to break free and check his descent was regarded as the loser; and the other—especially if he had switched off his field and prolonged the fall until the last possible second—was regarded as the winner, even though the winner often became the loser by virtue of misjudging his altitude and ending up in a wheelchair or on a marble slab.

Bombing was another game played on days when low cloud cover screened participants from the eyes of the law. The rules demanded that one should take up position in cloud above an aerial highway, switch off lift, and fall down through a stream of commuters, preferably without using the CG force to vector the descent in any way. The aim was to strike fear into the soul of the staid, ordinary flier on his way home from work, and that aim was usually achieved because anybody who thought objectively about the thing realised the impossibility of judging the closing angles well enough to guarantee there would never be a collision. On more than one occasion Hasson had shot pain-killing drugs into bomber and bombed alike, and had stood helplessly by while the Fifth Horseman had added fresh coffin-shaped symbols to his tally.

Werry activated his microphone. "Henry, have you got any IDs?"

"Some. The kid who did it checks out as a Martin Prada, with an address in Stettler." There was a moment of fretful near-silence from the radio. "He might have been holed up in the Chinook all morning. If there was a party up there last night they could be starting to get a bit restless. This low-level stratus we're getting swallowed up the hotel about an hour ago, so they're free to come and go as they please."

"What about the other guy?"

"All I know is he isn't local. Judging by his gear, he's up from the States."

"That's all we need," Werry said bitterly. "Any sign of drug abuse on the kid?"

"Al, he hit a light pole on the way down," the radio said in aggrieved tones. "I'm not about to start poking around in the mess looking for hypo marks."

"All right—I'll be there in a couple of minutes." Werry broke the radio connection and gave Hasson a sidelong glance. "If there's a US citizen involved it trebles the paperwork. How's that for bad luck?"

His or yours? Hasson thought. Aloud he said, "What's the narcotic situation like?"

"Most of the traditional stuff has died out, except for some acid, but empathin is getting to be a big problem." Werry shook his head as he leaned forward to scan the horizon. "That's the one that really beats me, Rob. I can understand kids wanting to get high, but wanting to get mixed up inside each other's heads, thinking the other guy's thoughts . . . You know, we get them down at the station some nights and for a couple of hours—till the stuff wears off, that is—they genuinely don't know who they are. Sometimes two of them give the same name and address. One of them actually believes he's the other one! Why do they do it?"

"It's a group thing," Hasson said. "Group identity has always been important to kids, and empathin makes it a reality."

"I leave all that stuff to the psychiatrists." Werry switched off his siren as a cluster of vehicles with flashing lights appeared on the road ahead. The outskirts of the city had been left behind and the country lay flat and white all around, looking as though it had been abandoned for ever. Parallel to the road but hundreds of metres above it were two bell-mouthed aerial tunnels, bilaser projections glowing yellow and magenta, which guided fliers who were entering or leaving the city. There was a steady flow of travellers within the insubstantial tubes, but others were swarming down through different levels of the cold air, drawn by the activity on the ground.

Werry brought the car to a halt near the others, got out and picked his way across the snow to a group of men which included two in police flying suits. On the ground, in the midst of the thicket of legs, were two objects covered by black plastic sheets. Hasson averted his eyes and thought determinedly about his television set while a man drew back the sheets to let Werry inspect what lay underneath. Werry talked to the others in the group for a minute, then came back to the car, opened the rear door and took out his flying suit.

"I've got to go aloft for a while," he said, pulling on the insulated one-piece garment. "Henry picked up a couple of blips on his radar and he thinks some of the punks might still be up there."

Hasson peered up at the all-obscuring cloud. "They're crazy if they are."

"I know, but we have to go up and fire off a few flares and stir things up a bit. Let the good citizens see us on the job." Werry finished zipping his suit and began to don his CG harness, looking tough and competent once more as he tightened the various straps. "Rob, I hate to ask you this, but could you take the car back across town and pick up my boy Theo coming out of school?"

"I should be able to cope if you give me directions."

"I wouldn't ask, but I promised him I'd be there."

"Al, there's no problem," Hasson said, wondering why the other man was being so diffident.

"There's a bit of a problem." Werry hesitated, looking strangely embarrassed. "You see . . . Theo is blind. You'll have to identify yourself to him."

"Oh." Hasson was lost for words. "I'm sorry."

"It isn't a permanent condition," Werry said quickly. "They're going to fix him up in a couple of years. He'll be fine in a couple of years."

"How will I recognise him?"

"There's no problem—it isn't a special school. Just look out for a tall boy carrying a sensor cane."

"That's all right." Hasson strove to absorb the instructions on how to reach the school and to guess in advance what sort of relationship he might have with a blind boy, and all the while he was reluctantly fascinated by Werry's preparations for flight, the instinctive rituals a professional never failed to observe before venturing into a perilous environment. All straps properly tightened and secured. Shoulder and ankle lights functioning. Fuel cells in good condition and delivering at the correct level. All the nets, lines and pouches associated with the air policeman's trade present and properly stowed. Suit heater functioning. Communications equipment functioning. Face plate locked in down position and helmet radar functioning. CG field generator warmed up and all controls on belt panel at correct preliminary settings.

Following the pre-flight checks with mind and eye, Hasson was lulled for a moment into visualising what came next—the effortless leap which became a dizzy ascent, the sensation of falling *upwards*, the patterns of fields and roads dwindling and wheeling below—and his stomach muscles contracted, propelling a sour bile into the back of his throat. He swallowed forcibly and distracted himself by sliding over behind the car's steering wheel and examining the controls.

"I'll see you back at the house," Werry said. "As soon as I can."

"See you," Hasson replied stolidly, refusing to pay much attention as Werry touched a control at his belt and was wafted upwards into the cold grey sky at the centre of an invisible sphere of energy, his own micro-universe in which some of the basic dictates of nature had been reversed. The two other cops took off at the same time, stiff-legged, heads tilted backwards as they made cautious ascents into an unnaturally crowded medium.

Hasson started the engine, made a three-point turn and drove back towards the city. The sky had darkened perceptibly as the cloud cover thickened, although it was still mid-afternoon, and the translucent pastel geometries of Tripletree's traffic control system were stark and garish at the upper edge of his field of vision. He found his way into the commercial centre without difficulty, aided by the fact that the city was entirely laid out on a simple grid pattern, and was leaving it again on the west side when he came to a snap decision about his craved-for television set. Slowing the car down, he began to study the store fronts which were drifting by and was rewarded by finding an electrical dealer within a matter of seconds. He parked just a few car lengths beyond the appliance-filled window and walked back to it, experiencing a tremulous joy over the prospect of being safe for that evening and all the evenings to come. The glass door refused to move for him when he tried the handle.

Hasson stepped back and stared at the lighted interior with disbelieving eyes, wondering how a downtown store—even a small one—could be closed so early in the day. He swore at his bad luck, feeling cheated and persecuted, then became aware of a man watching him from the window of the adjoining premises. Unwilling to give up his electronic talisman when it had almost been within his grasp, he entered the other store and discovered it specialised in health foods. The shelves were overloaded with packets and bottles, and the air was charged with conflicting yeasty, malty and herbal odours. Behind a cluttered counter was a small, middle-aged man of Asian descent who regarded Hasson with knowing, sympathetic eyes.

"Next door," Hasson said. "What's happening next door? Why is there nobody there?"

"Ben has stepped out for five minutes." The small man had a precise dry voice. "He'll be right back."

Hasson frowned and shifted from one foot to the other. "I can't wait. I'm supposed to be somewhere else."

"Ben will be back any minute, any second even. There'll be no delay, Mr. Haldane."

Hasson looked at the storekeeper in surprise. "How did you know my . . .?"

"You're driving Reeve Werry's car, and you speak with a British accent." The man's eyes developed a humorous twinkle. "Simple, isn't it? I keep passing up chances to be mysterious and inscrutable, but with a name like Oliver there's no point in my overdoing the Oriental bit, is there?"

Hasson eyed the small man sombrely, wondering if he was being ribbed. "Are you sure he'll be right back?"

"Positive. You can wait in here if you like."

"Thanks, but . . ."

"Perhaps I can sell you what you need."

The unusual phrasing, plus some indefinable quality in the store-keeper's voice, alerted the dormant cop in Hasson, making him wonder what might actually be on offer. His mind flicked over a list of possibilities—drugs, women, gambling facilities, contraceptives, stolen property—then he decided that nobody but a fool would proposition a relative of the local police chief on such a short acquaintanceship. And Oliver, whatever else he might be, was no fool.

"I don't need anything." Hasson picked up a small bottle of lime green pills, glanced incuriously at the label and set it back on the shelf. "I'd better go."

"Mr. Haldane!" Oliver's voice remained light, his manner easy, but his eyes disturbed Hasson. "Your life is entirely your own concern, but you are not at ease within yourself—and I can help. Believe me, I can help."

Good sales pitch, Hasson thought defensively. He was choosing words to cover his retreat when a burly, grey-haired man passed the store window and waved in at Oliver. Almost immediately there was the sound of the adjoining door being opened and Hasson started towards the street, relieved of the need to speak.

"So long, Mr. Haldane." Oliver smiled, looking compassionate rather than disappointed at the loss of a possible sale. "I hope you'll call again."

Hasson paused outside in the bitterly cold air, feeling he had had a narrow escape of some kind, and hurried into the electrical store. It took him less than five minutes to purchase a small solid-image television set, using some of the dollar currency which had been issued to him before he left England. He carried it out to the car, placed it carefully on the rear seat and resumed driving west-wards in the direction of the school. Its location became apparent from a distance because two tree-like bilaser projections linked it into the aerial traffic system. Hasson could see hundreds of tiny figures representing students and parents floating up the ruby-coloured outward stem and dispersing at different altitudes.

The school itself turned out to be a cluster of not-too-modern buildings surrounding a large take-off area and car park. Students and a scattering of teachers were still emerging from some of the doors, and the sight of them reassured Hasson that he was not late. He stopped the car and got out, with only a moderate twinge from his back, and looked around for Theo Werry. There were several knots of teenagers within a radius of fifty paces, each of them seething with playful energy as the young people responded to the open air and freedom from school restrictions.

Most of them seemed oblivious to anything outside their immediate areas, but he noticed that his arrival in the police cruiser had wrought a change in one group. Its members had drawn closer together for a few seconds and then reformed into a pattern which allowed a majority to observe his movements. Hasson's trained eye, without his bidding, detected the whispering and shuffling of feet and, above all, the slight preening movements of the shoulders which told him that young braves were entertaining thoughts of violence.

Sheer force of habit caused him to try assessing the command structure of the set, and he at once picked out a suited-up redhead of about eighteen—some four years older than his companions—who was standing in a slightly different attitude to the others and occasionally fingering his nostrils as he stared intently into the middle distance. *Why am I doing this?* Hasson thought, as he noted the heavily ornamented, non-standard straps of the man's CG harness and the faint rectangular markings on the flying suit which showed that its patches of fluorescent material had been removed to make the wearer harder to track in flight. The suit also looked wet, as though it had recently been worn in cloud. At that moment a younger member of the group turned towards him and Hasson experienced a nervous jangling in his stomach as he saw the slim white tube of a sensor cane in the boy's hand. He began walking in Hasson's direction, watched by his companions.

Hasson put on a smile of greeting and felt it dissolve into a novocaine numbness as he remembered it could not be seen. Theo Werry was a tall, black-haired boy with finely moulded features, pale skin and the beginnings of a moustache and beard shadow which signalled his approaching manhood. His eyes looked clear and normal, fully under control, and only the tilted-back angle of his head and an unnatural serenity of expression revealed that he was blind. Hasson felt a pang of combined rage and pity which raked him with its intensity, and his thoughts promptly seized on Al Werry's statement that the boy's condition was soon to be cured. He stood without moving as Theo approached him. The boy walked slowly but with assurance, angling his cane in such a way as to gain maximum information about Hasson's position and size from its invisible laser rays.

"Hello, Theo," Hasson said. "I'm Rob Haldane. Your father got called out on a job so he asked me to meet you."

"Hi." Theo made an adjustment to the ear piece which translated the signals from his cane into audio tones. He extended his left hand. Hasson gripped it with his own left, taking care to achieve a clean handshake.

"I'm sorry you've been troubled," Theo said. "I could have made it home by myself."

"It's no trouble." Hasson opened the passenger door of the police cruiser. "Would you like to get into the car?" He was surprised to see Theo shake his head.

"I'd prefer to fly back, if you don't mind. I've been cooped up all day."

"But . . ."

"It's all right," Theo said quickly. "I'm allowed to go up, as long as I'm tethered to another flier. You'll find my suit and harness in the trunk of the car."

"Your father didn't mention anything like that." Hasson began to feel uncomfortable. "He asked me to pick you up in the car."

"But it's all right—honestly. I often fly home from school." A note of impatience had crept into Theo's voice. "Barry Lutze has offered to go with me, and he's the best airman in Tripletree."

"Is that the redhead you were talking to?"

"That's him. The best flier in the country."

"Really?" Hasson glanced across the intervening ground at Lutze, who immediately turned away and began staring into the distance while he stroked his nostrils between finger and thumb.

Theo smiled. "Can I have my suit and harness, please?"

Hasson continued appraising Lutze while he came to a decision. "Sorry, Theo. I can't take that responsibility—not without your father's express consent. You can see my position, can't you?"

"Me? I can't see anything," Theo said bitterly. He found the car with his cane, got into it and sat down. Watched intently by the other boys, Hasson lowered himself into the driving seat and tried not to wince as the nerves in his back reacted violently to the flexure. He started the engine, drove away from the take-off area and turned towards the city. Theo maintained a reproachful silence.

"It's a lousy day for flying, anyway," Hasson said after a time. "Far too cold."

"The chinook can make it warmer up top."

"There's no chinook today—just low cloud and a katabatic wind falling down from the mountains. Believe me, you're better off out of it."

Theo showed signs of interest. "Do you fly a lot, Mr. Haldane?"

"Ah . . . no." Hasson realised he had made a mistake in reviving the subject of flying in the presence of a sky-struck boy. "I don't fly at all, as a matter of fact."

"Oh. I'm sorry."

"It's all right." The apology showed the boy felt a shameful admission had been made, and in spite of all the dictates of his common sense Hasson was suddenly unwilling to let the matter drop. "There's nothing wrong with travelling in comfort, you know."

Theo shook his head and spoke with bland certainty. "You've got to fly. When I can see again I'm going to *live* up there. It's the only way."

"Who says?"

"Barry Lutze, for one—and he knows. Barry says you can tell a good airman just by looking at him."

Hasson recognised a disturbing echo of the angels' creed, the unsystematic and semi-instinctive mode of thought—too primeval to be classed as a philosophy—which was born in the minds of some who flew like supermen far above the drowsing earth. It was a dangerous creed, and one he seemed to have been fighting for the whole of his life. He recalled noticing the condensation on Lutze's flying suit and once again, entirely without his volition, the policeman in him began to test patterns of ideas.

"Barry seems to tell you lots of things," he said. "Do you know him well?"

"Pretty well," Theo replied with simple pride. "He talks to me a lot."

"Was he doing a bit of cloud-running this afternoon?"

Theo's face altered. "Why do you want to know?"

"No special reason," Hasson said, realising he had given himself away. "I'm just interested. Was he aloft?"

"Barry spends most of his time aloft."

"It's not the sort of weather I'd pick to go drilling holes in clouds."

"Who said he was flying in cloud?"

"Nobody." Hasson, now anxious to abandon the subject, scanned the twin lines of unfamiliar buildings ahead of the car. "I'm not sure if I remember the way home from here."

"Is there a sort of brown glass building at the next intersection?" Theo said. "A furniture store with a projection of a big armchair on the roof?"

"Yes—just ahead of us."

"Make a left there and follow the road till you pick up the north freeway. It's a bit longer that way, but it's easier when you don't know the place too well."

"Thanks." Hasson carried out the instruction and glanced curiously at his passenger, wondering if Theo still possessed some degree of sight.

"I can just about tell night from day," Theo said, "but I've got a good memory."

"I wasn't going to . . ."

Theo smiled. "Everybody's surprised to find I'm not completely helpless. I keep a map of the city in my head and I check off my position on it. I move a little dot along the streets."

"That's really something." Hasson was impressed by the boy's fortitude.

"The system doesn't work in the air, that's all."

"No, but you'll be fine in a couple of years, won't you?"

Theo's smile hardened. "You've been talking to my father."

Hasson gnawed his lower lip, having learned yet again that Theo was a highly perceptive person with no interest in making small talk. "Your father did tell me you'd be having an operation or something like that in two years' time. Perhaps I picked him up wrong."

"No, you picked him up right," Theo said easily. "I've only got to wait another two years—and that's nothing, is it? Nothing at all."

"I wouldn't say that," Hasson mumbled, wishing the conversation had never got started, wishing he could be alone in his room, secure, with the door locked and the curtains drawn and all the world a television stage. He tightened his grip on the steering wheel and concentrated on following the traffic markers on the road which looped northwards around the outskirts of the city. The road passed through a cutting which enclosed it between steep snowy banks, shutting off all signs of habitation and creating the impression that he was driving in a wilderness.

Hasson was watching a slaty triangle of sky opening out to receive him when something struck the car with enough force to make it rock slightly on the suspension. The impact appeared to have been on the roof, but nothing that could have caused it bounced down on to the pavement.

Theo sat up straight. "What was that?"

"I think we've got company," Hasson said. He trod gently on the brake pedal and at the same instant a flier made a swooping descent to land on the road about a hundred metres ahead. The flier was a big man who was wearing a black suit, a harness with fluorescent orange straps and—in spite of the fading light conditions—mirror-lensed sun glasses. Hasson immediately recognised Buck Morlacher and made a simultaneous guess that his partner, Starr Pridgeon, was at that moment perched on the roof of the car, having matched velocities in the air and dropped on to it. A wave of irritation, rather than anger, caused him to react as his former self. The car was still losing speed gradually as it neared Morlacher, but Hasson kicked down on the brake and jolted the vehicle to a halt. A blue-suited figure tumbled down the sloping windshield, struck the nose of the car and slid the rest of the way down on to the road.

Hasson, now regretting his impulsive action, sat perfectly still as the figure sprang to its feet and he saw the thin, venomous face of Starr Pridgeon coming towards him. Pridgeon wrenched open the driver door and his eyes widened in surprise.

"Hey, Buck," he called. "This ain't Werry—it's his Goddamn cousin from Goddamn England."

Morlacher paused briefly, then continued his approach to the car. "I'll talk to him, anyway."

"Right." Pridgeon put his head right inside the car until his face was almost touching Hasson's. "What was the idea?" he whispered. "What was the idea puttin' me down on the road like that?"

Hasson, numb with apprehension, shook his head and somehow chose the exact words Pridgeon had used earlier when he had felled Al Werry. "It was a pure accident."

Pridgeon's expression became murderous. "You want me to drag you out of there?"

"It was an accident," Hasson said, gazing straight ahead. "I'm not used to this sort of car."

"If I thought you had enough . . ."

"Come out of there," Morlacher said to Pridgeon, appearing at his elbow. Pridgeon withdrew, scowling, walked round to the other side of the car and stared in at Theo Werry. The boy remained motionless, his face calm.

Morlacher stooped to look in at Hasson. "What's your name? Halford or something like that, isn't it?"

"It's Haldane."

Morlacher appeared to digest the information for a moment, the two triangles of red glowing on the pink background of his face. "Where's Werry?"

"Over on the east side," Hasson said, submitting to the interrogation. "There was an AC."

"A what?" Morlacher demanded suspiciously.

"An aerial collision. Two people dead. He had to be there."

"He should have been there *before* somebody got killed." Morlacher was speaking in tones of barely suppressed rage, a fact which Hasson noted and found slightly puzzling—Morlacher had not struck him as being particularly humanitarian or public spirited in his outlook. He was pondering the matter when he heard a click on his right and turned his head to see that Pridgeon had opened the passenger door and was peering in at Theo with a kind of brooding, clinical interest. Theo, although he must have heard the noise and felt the influx of cold air, did not move in any way.

Hasson tried to put aside the distraction. "It's hard to show up before an accident."

"Accident my ass," Morlacher growled. "That was no accident. Those hopped-up young punks get away with murder. We *let* them get away with murder."

"One of them got killed as well."

"You think that makes things right?"

"No." Hasson had to concede the point. "But it shows . . ."

"The other man who got hit wasn't just anybody, you know. He was an important visitor to our country. An important visitor—and look what happens to him!"

"Did you know him?" Hasson's attention was distracted from the subject of the dead flier by the fact that Pridgeon had spread one of his hands out and was holding it a bare centimetre away from Theo's nose. The boy sensed its presence almost at once and jerked his head back. Pridgeon's mouth twitched with amusement behind the wispy tendrils of his moustache and he repeated the experiment, this time holding his hand a little further away. Hasson stared down at his own hands gripping the steering wheel and tried to comprehend what Morlacher was saying.

". . . in all the media tonight," the big man thundered, "and what will the message be? I'll tell you what the message will be. They'll be saying it isn't safe to fly north of Calgary. They'll be saying this is cowboy country up here. I tell you, it's enough to make a man . . ." Morlacher's peg-like front teeth came together with an audible click, shutting off the flow of words as his anger went beyond the limits of articulation.

Hasson gazed up at him, mute, helpless, baffled, wondering what was coming next, wondering if the predatory strangers would resort to violence against a sick man and a blind boy. Beside him, Theo was rocking his head from side to side in an effort to escape the unseen proximity of Pridgeon's hand.

"When you see Werry tell him I've had enough," Morlacher said at last. "You tell him I'm full up to my back teeth with this sort of thing, and that I'm coming over to his place to see him. Got that?"

"I'll tell him," Hasson said, relieved to see that Morlacher's hand was now resting on the flight control panel on his belt.

"Come on, Starr—we've got work to do." Morlacher moved a

switch and was hurled upwards into the sky, disappearing from Hasson's restricted field of view in a fraction of a second. On the other side of the car, Pridgeon snapped his fingers loudly in Theo's face, causing the boy to flinch, then performed his intimidatory trick of suddenly fixing Hasson with a bleak, hostile stare. He backed away from the car, still staring, leaped upwards and was gone. There was a silence disturbed only by the flustering of the breeze in the car's open doors.

Hasson gave an uncertain laugh. "What was all that about?"

Theo compressed his lips, refusing to speak.

"It was nice of them to drop by and see us," Hasson said, trying to make light of his sense of inadequacy and shame. "Friendly people you have around here."

Theo put out his right hand, pulled the passenger door shut and shifted slightly in the seat, signalling that he wanted to go home. Hasson took a deep breath as he closed his own door and set the car rolling again. They emerged from the cutting. Scattered houses, some of them already showing lights, became visible far off to one side. In all other directions a vast unfamiliar land stretched away to the dimness where the snow was turning as grey as the sky. Hasson felt totally alone.

"I wasn't quite sure what to say back there," he ventured. "Only having been in town a few hours . . . not really knowing anybody . . . I wasn't quite sure how to handle the situation."

"It's all right," Theo replied. "You handled it exactly the way my father would have done."

Hasson weighed the comment and understood that he had been insulted, but he decided against trying to put up a defence. "I can't understand why Morlacher is so upset—is he the city mayor or something?"

"No, he's just our friendly local gangster."

"Then what's on his mind?"

"You'd better ask my father about that. He works for Morlacher, so he should know."

Hasson glanced at Theo and saw that his face was pale and stern. "That's going a bit far, isn't it?"

"You think so? All right, let's put it this way." Theo spoke with a bitterness which made him sound like a much older person. "Mr. Morlacher put my father into the reeve's job, and he did it because he knew he would be completely ineffectual. The idea was that Mr. Morlacher would be able to do anything he wanted around Tripletree without being inconvenienced by the law. Now the situation has changed and Mr. Morlacher needs some hard-nosing done on his behalf—and there's nobody to do it for him. I'm sure you can appreciate the humour in that. Everybody else in town does."

The boy's words came across like a carefully planned and rehearsed speech, one which had been repeated many times to many people, and Hasson realised he had dipped his toes into a deep dark pool of family relationships. Shocked though he was by Theo's cynicism, he made up his mind to backtrack before getting involved in other people's problems. He was in Canada for no other reason than to rest and recuperate, and at the end of his allotted time he was going to flit away, as free and unencumbered as a bird. Life, he had learned, was difficult enough . . .

"I think we'll be home in a few minutes," he said. "There's a road ahead which looks like the northbound motorway, freeway."

"Make a right there, then take the third on the right," Theo replied, an odd inflection in his voice making him sound almost disappointed over Hasson's failure to respond to his set piece. He changed his position in the seat several times, looking moody and intelligent, giving the impression that his mind was far from being at ease.

"The accident this afternoon," he said. "Was it a bad one?"

"Bad enough—two people dead."

"Why was Mr. Morlacher talking about murder?"

Hasson slowed down at the intersection. "As far as I know some mental subnormals started bombing the east approach—with the inevitable result."

"Who says it's inevitable?"

"A character called Isaac Newton. If somebody is crazy enough to switch off in mid-air it only takes him seven seconds to reach terminal velocity of two hundred kilometres an hour, and no matter what sort of vector he tries to add . . ." Hasson paused as he became aware of Theo's unseeing eyes being turned towards him. "We get to know about that sort of thing in the insurance business."

"I suppose you would," Theo said thoughtfully.

Hasson fell silent, wondering if the stories he had heard about the uncanny perceptiveness of some blind people could be true. He followed the directions given him by Theo and brought the car to a halt outside Al Werry's house. Theo made an adjustment to the controls on his cane, bringing life to the inset ruby beads, got out of the car and began walking towards the house. Hasson lifted his television set out of the rear seat and followed him, glad to turn his back on the darkening world.

The hall seemed smaller than before due to the fact that Theo was struggling out of his coat in the centre of it, and this time the aroma of coffee had been added to the background smells of wax polish and camphor. Hasson's anxiety level increased at the prospect of having to go into the back room, there and then, and sit making conversation with a group of near-strangers. He made immediately for the stairs, fighting off the urge to go up them two at a time before the door to the back room was opened.

"Tell your folks I've gone up to unpack," he said to Theo in a low voice. "Then I'm going to freshen up a bit."

He reached the landing just as the sound of a door handle turning came from below. He made a panicky rush into his own room, set the television on the bed and locked the door behind him. The room looked dim and strange in the twilight. Faces in framed photographs stared at each other in silent communication, agreeing among themselves that the intruder in their midst should be ignored. Hasson drew the curtains together, switched on a light and busied himself with setting up the television on a table beside the bed. He switched it on, bringing into existence a miniature proscenium under which tiny human figures strutted and strove in a perfect simulation of life.

Hasson doused the light, hurriedly stripped off his outer clothing and—with his eyes fixed on the technicoloured microcosm—got into the bed. He pulled the covers up until they almost covered his head, creating yet another barrier between himself and the universe outside. The coolness of the bedding coming into contact with his back produced painful spasms which caused him to twist and turn for a full minute, but eventually he was able to find a comfortable position and begin relaxing his guard. Using the remote control panel, he instructed the set to sample any British television programmes that were available by satellite and promptly discovered that, due to the difference in time zones, he had access to nothing but early morning educational broadcasts. In the end he settled for a holofilm that was being put out by a local station and promised himself he would go back to the store at the first opportunity and buy some library spools of British situation comedies and drama series. In the meantime, he felt warm, tolerably secure, free from pain, absolved from the need to act or think . . .

Hasson was recalled from his electronic demi-world by a persistent tapping on the bedroom door. He eased himself into an upright position and surveyed the room, which was now in darkness, reluctant to leave the cocoon of bedding. The tapping noise continued. Hasson got to his feet, went to the door and opened it to find Al Werry advancing upon him, still in full uniform.

"You can't see a thing in here," Werry commented, switching on the lights as he spoke. "Were you asleep?"

"Resting, anyway," Hasson said, blinking.

"Good idea—you'll be in good shape for the party tonight."

Hasson felt something lurch in his chest. "What party?"

"Hey! I see you went ahead and got yourself a TV." Werry crossed to the television and hunkered down to examine it, a doubtful expression appearing on his face. "Dinky little thing, isn't it? When you get used to a two-metre job like the one we have down in the front room anything else hardly seems worth bothering with."

"Did you say something about a party?"

"Sure thing. It won't be too big—just a few friends coming round to meet you and have a few drinks—but I promise you, Rob, you'll get a real Albertan welcome. You're really going to enjoy yourself."

"I . . ." Hasson gazed into Werry's eager face and realised the impossibility of putting him off. "You shouldn't have gone to any trouble."

"It's no trouble—specially after the way you guys looked after me in England."

Hasson made another attempt to recall their first meeting, the drinking session which Werry appeared to cherish in his memory, but no images were forthcoming and he felt an obscure guilt. "I met up with your friend Morlacher this afternoon, by the way."

"Is that a fact?" Werry looked unconcerned.

"He said the man who got killed today was some kind of a VIP."

"Bull! He was a buyer for a department store down in Great Falls. He didn't deserve to get killed, of course, but he was just an ordinary joe up here on an ordinary business trip. Another statistic."

"Then why did . . .?"

"Buck always talks that way," Werry said, losing some of his composure. "He's got it into his head that the Civil Aviation Authority can be talked into extending the north-south air corridor up past Calgary to Edmonton, maybe even as far as Athabasca itself. He goes on TV, gets up petitions, brings bigwigs here out of his own pocket . . . Doesn't seem to realise there just isn't enough urgent freight traffic to justify the expense."

Hasson nodded, visualising the cost of installing a chain of automatic radar posts, energy fences and manned patrol stations to bring a three-hundred-kilometre strip up to the safety standards demanded by the various pilots' guilds. "What's it to him, anyway?"

"The Chinook. The big lolly. The inn on a pin." Werry paused to look affronted. "Buck thinks he can still get some of his old man's money back out of it. He sees it as a luxury airport hotel, convention centre, billion dollar brothel, Olympic games stadium, the United Nations building, Disney planet, last filling station before Mars . . . You name it—Buck thinks he's got it."

Hasson gave a sympathetic smile, recognising the kind of bitter rhetoric used by men suffering from the age-old complaint of a thorn in the side. "He was worked up about it this afternoon."

"What does he expect me to do?"

"From what I can gather, he's coming over to tell you what he expects. I told him I'd pass the word on."

"Thanks." Werry furrowed the carpet with the toe of a glossy boot. "Sometimes I wish I'd . . ." He glanced at Hasson from under lowered brows and suddenly smiled, resuming the guise of the insouciant revolutionary colonel. His fingers traced the pencil line of his moustache as though making sure it was still in place.

"Listen, Rob, we've got better things to talk about," he said. "You came here to forget about police work and I'm going to make sure you do. I want you to report downstairs in thirty minutes, spruced up for a party and thirsty as hell. Got it? Got it?"

"I probably could use a drink," Hasson said. Too much had happened to him in one day and he knew from experience that it would take at least a quarter-litre of whisky to guarantee an easy descent into sleep and no dreams of flying.

"That's more like my boy." Werry slapped him on the shoulder and left the room in a flurry of air currents which were scented with a peculiar mixture of talc, leather and machine oil.

Hasson glanced regretfully at the bed and the comfortably glowing television set, then began to do some belated unpacking. Dreadful though the prospect of a party was, it offered him more leeway than an evening cooped up with Al Werry and the three other members of his household. It should be possible for him to get into a corner near the booze supply and sit tight until he could decently retire for the night. That way he would have won through to the next day, when he could think about regrouping his forces to withstand fresh onslaughts.

He gathered up his toiletries, opened the bedroom door a fraction and listened to make sure there was no chance of encountering May or Ginny Carpenter, then set out with stealthy tread towards the bathroom. Part way along the landing he reached another door which was slightly ajar, and was intrigued to see that the room beyond was being alternately lit up and plunged into total darkness every few seconds. Hasson hurried on by, went into the bathroom and spent fifteen minutes on having a shower and generally making himself presentable. He renewed an earlier finding that it is always a stranger who looks back at one from a strange mirror. The only explanation he could think of was that people who are familiar with the positioning of their mirrors unconsciously pose, straining towards a desired image of themselves, before turning towards their reflections.

In this case, Hasson was taken unawares by the sight of a dark-haired, unobtrusively muscular man whose face was marred by an apprehensive tautness around the mouth and eyes. He stood at the mirror consciously composing his features, trying to eliminate the traces of strain and self-pity he saw there, then left the bathroom and went back along the landing. The intermediate door was still ajar and the light was still flashing on and off behind it. Hasson passed by, but immediately was troubled by fears of some bizarre electrical fault which could ignite the dry timber of the house. He went back, eased the door open a little further and looked into the room. Theo Werry was sitting cross-legged on the bed, holding a table lamp directly in front of his eyes and steadily operating the switch. Hasson backed away as silently as possible and returned to his room, filled with the shameful realisation that there were worse injuries than ruptured spinal disks and broken bones.

Moving slowly and thoughtfully, he dressed in comfortable slacks and a soft maroon shirt, and by the time he had finished guests had begun to arrive for the party. Their voices came up through the floor in irregular waves. They were loud, relaxed and cheerful, as befitted members of the exclusive club for those who felt at home in Al Werry's house—a club to which Hasson did not belong. He opened the bedroom door three times and turned back three times before mustering enough resolve to go downstairs.

The first person he saw on entering the front room was May Carpenter, now dressed in a few scraps of white diaphanous material held together by fine gold chains. She turned towards him, smiling, almost swamping him with a composite projection of every screen sex goddess he could bring to mind. He blinked, trying to absorb the visual impact, then became aware of other women in similarly exotic attire and men in colourful braided jackets. It dawned on him that, contrary to the impression he had received from Werry, the occasion was one for dressing up. *Everybody,* a silent voice reprimanded, *is looking at you.* He hesitated in the doorway, wondering if there was any way in which he could withdraw.

"There he is," Al Werry shouted. "Come in and meet the gang, Rob." Werry came to him, glass in hand, incongruously dressed in his reeve's uniform minus only the tunic and cap. He gripped Hasson's elbow and led him towards the others.

Lost for something to say, Hasson glanced down at Werry's uniform. "Are you on call tonight?"

Werry looked surprised. "Of course not."

"I just thought . . ."

"Say hello to Frank and Carol," Werry put in and then went on to perform a bewildering series of introductions from which Hasson failed to salvage even one name. Numbed by the succession of smiles, handshakes and amiable greetings, Hasson arrived like a piece of flotsam at a table of drinks presided over by Ginny Carpenter, who was wearing the same coppertex suit he had seen her in earlier. She gazed at him without moving, implacable as a suit of armour.

"Give the man a drink," Werry said, chuckling. "That's Rob's special brand—the Lockhart's. Give him a good belt."

Ginny picked up the bottle, examined its label critically and poured out a small measure. "Anything with it?"

"Soda water, thanks." Hasson accepted the glass and, under Werry's benign scrutiny, swallowed most of its contents. He was unable to prevent himself flinching as he discovered the whisky had been diluted with tonic water.

"All right, is it?" Werry said. "It took me days to track down that bottle."

Hasson nodded. "It's just that I never tried it with tonic water before."

Expressions of incredulity and delight appeared on Werry's face. "Don't tell me Ginny gave you the wrong mixer! What a woman!"

"He oughta be drinking good rye and ginger ale, same as everybody else," Ginny said unrepentantly, and Hasson knew she had ruined his drink on purpose. Baffled and depressed by her hostility, he turned away and stood without speaking until Werry had furnished him with a fresh glass, which this time was brimming with almost-neat whisky. He moved into a quiet corner and began working on his drink, methodically and joylessly, hoping to anaesthetise himself down to a level at which the nearness of strangers would be unimportant.

The party went on all about him, forming and dissolving different centres of activity, gradually growing louder in proportion to the amount of alcohol consumed. Al Werry, apparently feeling he had discharged all his obligations to Hasson, circulated continuously among his friends, never staying more than a few seconds with any one group, looking healthy, spruce and competent—and totally out of place—in his chocolate-brown uniform. May Carpenter spent most of the time surrounded by at least three men, seeming to be fully absorbed in responding to their attention and yet always managing to intercept his gaze when he looked in her direction. It came to him that Werry and May had one thing in common in that their characters were completely impenetrable as far as he was concerned. In each case the physical presence was so overwhelming as to obscure the inner being. May, for example, was behaving exactly as if she found Hasson interesting, in spite of the fact that he had virtually ceased to exist as far as women were concerned. Perhaps she had a strong maternal instinct; perhaps she met all men on the same terms—Hasson had no way to tell. He toyed with the problem at odd moments between bouts of conversation with men and women who took it in turns to relieve his solitude. The noise level in the room continued to increase. Hasson persevered with his drinking until he had finished the half-bottle of Scotch and was obliged to try the rye, which he found bland but reasonably acceptable.

At one stage in the evening, when the lights had been turned down and a number of people were dancing, he made the discovery that the chubby, apple-cheeked young man talking to him was not a farmer, as his appearance suggested, but was actually a physician called Drew Collins. A memory which Hasson had suppressed—that of Theo Werry sitting alone in his room with the table lamp held close to his eyes—sprang to the forefront of his consciousness.

"I'd like to ask you something," he said, uncertain about the ethics involved. "I know it's the wrong time and all that . . ."

"Don't worry about all that crap," Drew said comfortably. "I'd write you a prescription on a beer mat."

"It isn't about myself—I was wondering if you were Theo's doctor."

"Yeah, I look after young Theo."

"Well . . ." Hasson swirled his drink, creating a conical depression in its surface. "Is it true that he'll get his sight back in two years?"

"Perfectly true. Slightly less than two years, in fact."

"Why does the operation have to wait so long?"

"It isn't an operation as such," Drew explained, apparently happy to talk shop. "It's the culmination of a three-year course of treatment. The condition Theo suffers from is known as complicated cataract, which doesn't mean the cataract itself is complicated—just that there were other factors involved in his getting it so young. Until about twenty years ago there was only one possible treatment—removal of the opaque lenses—which would have left him with highly abnormal vision for life, but now we can restore the transparency of the lens capsule. It involves putting drops in the eyes every day for three years, but at the end of that time the simple injection of a tailored enzyme into the lenses will make them like new. It's a genuine medical advance."

"It certainly sounds that way," Hasson said. "Except . . ."

"Except what?"

"Three years is a long time to be left in the dark."

Unexpectedly, Drew moved closer to Hasson and lowered his voice. "Did Sybil rope you in, as well?"

Hasson stared at him in silence for a moment, trying to hide his confusion. "Sybil? No, she didn't rope me in."

"I thought she might have done," Drew said in confidential tones. "She contacted some of Al's relations and got them to lean on him, but Al's the only one who is legally responsible for the boy, and it had to be his own private, personal decision."

Hasson searched his memory and dredged up a vague recollection of Werry mentioning that his former wife's name was Sybil. A glimmer of partial understanding appeared in his mind.

"Well," he said guardedly, "there are things for and against this new treatment."

Drew shook his head. "The only thing against it is the three-year delay, but—especially for a youngster—that's a small price to pay for perfect vision."

"Is it?"

"Of course it is. Al made the decision, anyway, and Sybil should have stuck with him over it and backed him up, if only for Theo's sake. Personally, taking everything into consideration, I think he made the right decision."

"I suppose . . ." Hasson, recognising dangerous conversational waters ahead, cast around for a change of subject and for no reason he could explain his mind fastened on the man he had encountered in the downtown health food shop. "Do you get much competition from alternative medicine around here?"

"Practically none." Drew glanced sideways and raised his eyebrows as he was joined by Ginny Carpenter. "Albertan law is pretty strict about that sort of thing. Why do you ask?"

"It's nothing much. I bumped into an interesting character today—an Asian who runs a health food shop. He said his name was Oliver."

"Oliver?" Drew looked blank.

"That's Olly Fan," Ginny put in, cackling like a Disney witch.

"You wanna stay away from him, boy. You wanna stay away from all those Chinks. They can live where white folks would die off 'cause all they ever think about is how to make money." She swayed for a moment, glass in hand, her triangular face flushed with alcohol. "Do you wanna know how those sons make money in their corner stores when there's no customers in?"

"What I want is another drink," Drew replied, moving off.

Ginny caught his arm. "I'll tell you what they do. They can't bear to let a minute pass without making money, so they just stand there at the cigar counter opening match boxes and taking one match out of each. I've looked in and seen them at it—just standing there! One match out of each box! Nobody would ever miss one, but when they've done it fifty times they've got an extra box to sell. White folks wouldn't go to all that trouble, but the Chinks just stand there . . . One match out of each box!"

Hasson considered the story briefly, classified it under the heading of 'Racist Apocryphal' and simultaneously picked out a flaw in its internal logic. "Hard to believe, isn't it?"

Ginny mulled over his words and seemed to note their ambivalence. "Do you think I made all that up?"

"I didn't mean to imply . . ." Hasson smiled apologetically, dreading a confrontation with the flinty little woman. "I think I need another drink, too."

Ginny waved expansively in the direction of the table. "Go ahead and soak it up, friend."

Hasson thought of a number of retorts ranging from the coldly sarcastic to the crudely obscene, but again in his mind there was a verbal log-jam complicated by undercurrents of embarrassment, exhaustion and fear. He found himself mumbling thanks to Ginny and backing away from her like a courtier excusing himself from a royal presence. He topped up his glass, aware that he was drinking too much, and decided to adopt Werry's technique of continually moving from one locus to another until he could decently withdraw to the fortress of his room. In a short time the excess of strong drink combined with his tiredness to produce in him a trance-like state in which the room became an encompassing screen upon which human forms were flat and meaningless projections, like the patterns radiated by a guttering fire.

At one stage Hasson was dumbfounded to realise he had been

drawn into some kind of inebriated game whose rules were never made clear to him, but which engendered a great deal of stumbling in darkness, whispering, laughing, and slamming of unseen doors. It came to him that his chance to escape had arrived, that with any luck at all he could be safe in bed before his absence was even noticed. He tried to take his bearings in the darkness and set out for the door which opened into the hall, but his progress was impeded by others who seemed to possess a magical ability to know exactly what they were doing and exactly where they were going in the absence of light. A door opened in front of him, revealing a dimly-lit room, and several hands pushed Hasson forward. He heard the door slam behind him and in the same moment became aware that he was alone in the kitchen with May Carpenter. His heart began an unsteady pounding.

"Well, this *is* a surprise," she said in a low voice, coming towards him. "What sign have you got?"

"Sign?" Hasson stared at her in bewilderment. In the low-centred mellow light her flimsy party clothing appeared hardly to exist at all, turning her into a feverish erotic vision.

"Yes. I've got Libra." She held up a card with a drawing of a pair of scales. "What have you got?"

Hasson spread the fingers of his right hand and looked down at it. He was holding a card which also bore the sign of Libra.

"The same," May said. "That's lucky for both of us." With no trace of hesitation she put her arms around his neck, drawing his face down to meet hers. In the instant before the kiss Hasson saw her open mouth grow large with its nearness, large as any screen goddess's mouth in photographic close-up, as simplified and idealised as any sex symbol's mouth on a movie poster, all flawless mathematical curvatures and billowing crimson and stepped white planes, filling his eyes. During the kiss he experienced a sense of unreality, but at the same time his hands and body were receiving other messages, reminding him that the business of life was life and that it had not done with him yet. The revelation unnerved him with its forcefulness and simplicity, driving him to separate himself from May so that he could look at her again.

"This is good," he said, desperate for time in which to think, "but I'm very tired—I have to go to bed now."

"Perhaps it's just as well," May replied with a husky candour which Hasson found infinitely flattering and thrilling.

"Please excuse me." He turned, managed to identify the door which led directly into the hall and went through it. The hall was empty and in darkness, but somebody had used the bulging coat-stand as a support for a flying suit which had been left with the helmet in place and the shoulder and ankle lights flashing. Hasson squeezed past the golem-figure, went upstairs to his room and locked its door behind him. He went to the window, parted the curtains and looked out at the unfamiliar nightland. Snow was sifting down from the overhanging darkness. Immediately outside the window was a large, bare tree through the twigs of which a street lamp shed its radiance in concentric frosty circles. Myriads of glimmers, sparkles and reflections seemed to have been carefully placed on tangents to the circles, creating the sense of looking down a long illuminated tunnel wound with gossamer.

Hasson surveyed the view for perhaps a minute, trying to come to terms with the realisation that he had first seen it only twelve hours earlier, that he had completed less than a day of rest and recuperation. His mind was swollen with newly implanted memories of faces, voices, names and ideas as he went to the bed, stripped off his clothing and put on his pyjamas. As was usual at night, he was moving easily and without discomfort—the prolonged spell of activity having freed his joints and muscles—but it was time for his nightcap of pain.

He lay down on the bed and as soon as his back, now unprotected by day clothing, came in contact with the mattress a war began. The conflict was between various muscle groups, to see which would gain the advantage in new states of relaxation or tension, to see which could fire the greatest salvoes of agony—and in every case the loser was Hasson. He endured the struggle in silence until the spasms became infrequent, and very soon after that he had fallen asleep, a wounded warrior, exhausted, defeated in every skirmish of the day.

CHAPTER 4

THE DREAM WAS a familiar dream—the recreation of one day of Hasson's early life, the reliving of one event. One special event.

The preparations had been going on for days without his admitting, even to himself, what lay in the back of his mind. At first there had been an aerial tour of the Hebrides, and there was nothing very unusual in the fact that he had chosen to go alone. Then had come the procurement of extra power packs and special long-life oxygen bottles—but even that could have been interpreted as the taking of reasonable precautions prior to flying over a remote and sparsely populated area. And Hasson had actually begun his big climb before he finally acknowledged what he was doing.

It is in the nature of some men that when a machine is placed into their hands they have to satisfy themselves as to the limits of its performance. The CG harness operated by distorting gravitic field lines in such a way that the wearer could "fall" upwards—the closest analogy being that of a magnetic field in which any nodal point moved towards the region of greatest flux intensity. Because it drew most of its energy from the gravity field itself, the CG harness was most efficient at low altitudes. Close to the ground there was little drain on the power pack, but when a flier went high he found that his energy supplies were being squandered at greater and greater rates to compensate for inherent system inefficiency.

The most obvious consequence was that there was a limit to the altitude a personal flier could achieve, but—as is always the case—that limit could be modified by various technical and human factors. Air Policeman Robert Hasson, newly qualified for the force, had no more than a normal interest in the mechanics of the big climb. He had, however, a restless craving to explore his own psychological parameters, to find out which had the greater operational ceiling—the man or the machine. He knew it was an obsessional state of mind, that it was far from being novel or unusual, and yet the experiment had to be performed . . .

He lifted off from the Eye Peninsula on Lewis at dawn on a summer day and set his initial rate of climb at 250 metres a minute. The speed was fairly moderate by CG standards, but Hasson's dead weight had been greatly increased by the addition of three extra power packs and he had no wish to overload any of the equipment upon which his life depended. The maximum load which could be lifted by a CG harness was limited by the fact that, above a certain point, the load itself began to generate a noticeable gravitic field, thus interfering with the delicately arranged pattern of force lines set up by the counter-gravity unit. Basic modular mass, as the load figure was referred to in textbooks, was 137.2 kilogrammes, and exceeding it induced an effect known as field collapse, which gave the flier all the aerodynamic properties of a millstone.

Not sacrificing any energy by introducing horizontal components into his flight, Hasson allowed a light westerly wind to carry him out over the waters of the North Minch. Complex vistas of land and water continued to unfurl on all sides as the Scottish coast came into view some sixty kilometres to the east. The vegetation on the islands and mainland glowed in pastel shades in the early morning sun, with swaths of pale powdery yellow sifting into areas of lime green. Coastlines were limited with white against the nostalgic travel-poster blue of the ocean, and the air Hasson was breathing felt prehistoric in its cleanliness.

Twenty minutes after take-off he had reached a height of five kilometres, far above the levels normally used in personal flight. He sealed the faceplate of his helmet and began to draw on his bottled oxygen. Beneath the soles of his boots the rolling Earth was immense, beginning to show hints of curvature, and Hasson felt the first stirrings of loneliness. He could see no birds, no ships, no signs of human habitation in all the atlas-page sweeps of territory below—and there was no sound. Hasson was alone in the silent blue reaches of the sky.

Forty minutes after take-off he had reached a height of ten kilometres and knew he was passing through the level of the polar tropopause. The air around him had been steadily growing colder throughout his ascent, the temperature decreasing by six degrees or more with every kilometre of altitude, but now he could expect it to remain constant or even become slightly warmer as he penetrated the stratosphere. Unfortunately, that fact signified little real benefit for Hasson. His heavy-duty suit heaters were labouring to cope with a surrounding air temperature of almost fifty degrees below zero, and would go on being a major drain on his energy supply.

Ten minutes later Hasson saw a layer of thin cloud moving eastwards beneath him, beginning to obscure his view of the land, and he knew the time had come to perform the illegal action which had necessitated his making the flight from such a remote area. He checked his first power pack, saw that it was nearing exhaustion, and switched to the second in line. For one heart-stopping instant, while the electrical circuit was being broken and re-made, he felt himself begin to fall, but the harness renewed its grip on him almost immediately and he knew the ascent was continuing. He unbuckled the expended power unit and, with a transient pang of guilt, released it from his fingers. The heavy pack dwindled out of sight beneath his feet, bombing its way down to an unseen impact with the choppy waters of the Minch.

Hasson's plan had included shedding the second power unit and perhaps the third, provided conditions had been right, so as to lighten the load on those remaining as they clawed their way up into regions of weakening gravitic flux. A prime requisite, though, had been perfect visibility below. The chances of a falling unit causing any damage to life or property were virtually nonexistent in his present geographical location, but a deep-rooted instinct would not let him consider dropping a dense object through cloud. He would simply have to accept the limitation on his flight.

The realisation came as less of a disappointment than Hasson might have expected an hour earlier. He had already climbed higher than most fliers even cared to think about, and the nameless hunger within him was slowly abating. On the other hand, he had reached a dimensionless zone—once the domain of the big jets—and going on upwards into regions of darker blue seemed just as logical and natural as returning to the ancient kingdoms of men. With his head tilted back, and arms and legs trailing limply,

Hasson continued his climb, his posture an unconscious echo of the one in which mediaeval artists depicted human souls ascending to heaven. A single point of light—possibly Venus—appeared in the aching purity above him, beckoning, and Hasson swam towards it.

His rate of ascent was decreasing with every minute, in inverse proportion to the drain on his power packs, but a further hour took him to an altitude of twenty-five kilometres. The world curved away beneath him in nacreous splendour. There was no visible movement anywhere, except for the hastening progression of needles across the dials on his chest panel. Hasson flew onwards.

At thirty kilometres above sea level he checked his instruments and saw that his upward movement had all but ceased. His CG field generator, with less and less invisible grist for its mills, was expending stored energy at a prodigious rate simply to keep him from falling. The only way in which he could gain more height would be to discard the dead power packs, but he had ruled that action out, and in any case the result would be of no great significance. He had done what he set out to do.

Hanging motionless in the icy blue solitude, poised on the threshold of space, Hasson gazed all about him and felt . . . *nothing.* There was no fear, no elation, no wonder, no sense of achievement, no communion with the cosmos—removed from the context of humanity he had lost his humanity.

He completed a full survey of the heavens, knew himself to be a stranger there, then adjusted a control on his belt and began the long and lonely fall to Earth.

CHAPTER 5

HASSON AWOKE TO a room which was brilliant with diffused sunlight and he knew without looking at his watch that he had slept late. His head was throbbing so powerfully that he could actually hear the squirting pulses in the temple which was pressed into the pillow, and his tongue felt like stiffened chamois leather. There was also a fierce pressure in his bladder as a result of alcoholic enhancement of his body's diuretic processes.

Not a hangover, he protested to the morning. *The last thing I need is a hangover.* He lay still for a time, reacquainting himself with the room, wondering what had happened on the previous day to trigger the nervy fluttering of excitement he could feel at the threshold of consciousness. There was pleasure involved—that much he knew—the pleasure of . . . Hasson closed his eyes momentarily as a picture of May Carpenter came into focus in his mind, quickly followed by all the recriminations and objections appropriate to his age, background and temperament. She was too young; she was mated to his host; he was fantasising like an adolescent boy; she was not his type; it was highly unlikely that she could have any interest in him whatsoever—but, *but,* she had looked at him in a certain way, and she had said, "That's lucky for both of us," and she had said, "Perhaps it's just as well," and the fact that he had never actually communicated with her and had no knowledge of her as a person was not very important, because there was an abundance of time in which to . . .

A sudden renewal of the pressure in his abdomen brought Hasson to his senses, making it clear that he had to face the task of getting himself into an upright attitude after many hours of lying in bed. The first stage in the operation was to transfer himself, still in the horizontal position, from the bed to the floor, because he was tackling an engineering job of Brunelian magnitude and the first requirement was a firm and immovable base. He began by dragging his legs sideways to the edge of the mattress by hand, then he rolled over, grasped the underlying frame and drew himself into a kind of a controlled fall to the floor. The inevitable flexure of his back and the abrupt change of temperature initiated a period of torment which he bore in near-silence, staring at the ceiling through slitted eyes. When the spasms began to subside he rolled again until he was lying in the prone position and could begin the slow process—largely guided by trial and error—of raising his upper body and very carefully, like a mason inserting props to hold an unwieldy mass of stone, bringing more and more of his skeleton under it until he had achieved verticality.

Two minutes after making the decision to rise, Hasson was on his feet—breathing heavily, chastened by what he had just been through, but now capable of movement. He shuffled about the room, putting on a dressing gown and collecting toilet articles, then listened at the bedroom door to satisfy himself that opening it would not precipitate the ordeal of having to speak to strangers. The landing was deserted and the upper part of the house had an empty feel to it, although there were muted sounds of activity from below. In the bathroom he brushed his teeth and made the depressing discovery that two mouth ulcers he had thought to be fading away were more painfully active than before. Returning to the bedroom, he contemplated the idea of getting under the covers again and switching on the television, but the dehydration of his system had given him a powerful yearning for tea or coffee which could not be denied. He dressed and made his way down to the kitchen, wondering how he would react if he found May there alone. He tapped the door gently, went inside and saw Theo Werry seated by himself at the circular table, eating a dish of cereal. The boy was wearing slacks and a red sweater, and there was a pensive expression on his handsome young face.

"Morning, Theo," Hasson said. "No school today?"

Theo shook his head. "This is Saturday."

"I'd forgotten. The days don't seem to mean much to me now that . . ." Hasson checked himself and glanced around the room. "Where is everybody?"

"Dad's outside clearing snow. The other two have gone into town." Theo's choice of phrase and a certain dryness of tone informed Hasson that he did not care much for May or her mother.

"In that case, I'll brew myself some coffee," Hasson said. "I don't suppose anybody will mind."

"I'll do it for you, if you like." Theo half-rose from his chair, but Hasson persuaded him to go on with his breakfast. While performing the domestic routine of making the coffee he spoke to the boy about his tastes and pursuits, discovering as he did so that conversation with Theo was less of a strain on him than trying to exchange pleasantries with adults. They talked briefly about music and Theo's face became animated as he learned that Hasson shared his liking for Chopin and Liszt, as well as for some modern composers working for hard-toned piano.

"I suppose you listen to the radio a lot," Hasson said, sitting down with his coffee, and realised at once that he had made a mistake.

"That's what everybody supposes." Theo's voice had grown stony. "It's fun being blind as long as you have a radio."

"Nobody thinks that."

"But it's supposed to be a great solace, isn't it? Everywhere I go people turn on radios for me, and I never listen to them. I don't enjoy being blind—unsighted, they call it at school—and nobody's going to make me look like I'm enjoying it."

"That's a great bit of corkscrew logic," Hasson said gently, all too aware of his own stumblings under the burden of illness.

"I guess it is—but then a wood-louse isn't a very logical creature."

"Wood-louse? You've lost me, Theo."

The boy gave a humourless smile which saddened Hasson. "There's a Kafka story about a man who woke up one morning and found he had turned into a giant cockroach. It horrifies everybody that one, the idea of being turned into a cockroach—but if he'd really wanted to sick people off Kafka should have made the guy into a wood-louse."

"Why's that?"

"They're blind and they're busy. I've always hated those things because they're blind and so *busy.* Then I woke up one morning and found I'd been turned into a giant wood-louse."

Hasson stared at the black, vapouring liquid in his cup. "Theo, take some advice from a leading expert on the gentle art of beating oneself on the head with a club—don't do it."

"Mine's the only head I can get at."

"It was rough on your father too, you know—he's having a bad time as well."

Theo tilted his head and considered Hasson's remark for a few seconds. "Mr. Haldane," he said thoughtfully, "you don't know my father at all. I don't think you're really his cousin, and I don't think you're really an insurance salesman."

"That's funny," Hasson parried, "that's what my boss used to say to me every month when he looked at my figures."

"I'm not joking."

"He used to say that as well, but I surprised him by inventing a new kind of policy which let people insure themselves against being uninsured."

Theo's lips twitched. "I read a story once about a character called Nemo the Nameless."

Hasson chuckled, impressed by the speed with which the boy had classified his absurdity and correctly matched it. "You sound like another Stephen Leacock buff."

"No, I don't think I ever heard of him."

"But he was a Canadian humorist! The very best!" Hasson was mildly surprised to find he could be enthusiastic about anything connected with literature—for months he had been unable even to open a book.

"I'll try to remember the name," Theo said.

Hasson tapped him lightly on the back of the hand. "Listen, I'm about due to re-read some Leacock. If I pick up a couple of books perhaps I could read them to you. What do you say?"

"That sounds all right. I mean, if you have the time . . ."

"I've got loads of time, so we'll make it definite," Hasson said, musing on the fact that immediately he had started thinking about doing something for somebody else his own state of mind had improved. It seemed there was a lesson to be learned. He sipped his coffee, wincing occasionally as the hot fluid came in contact with a mouth ulcer, and tacitly encouraged Theo to talk about anything that came into his mind, as long as it had nothing to do with Hasson's past and his supposed family connections with Al Werry. Theo's interest in flying quickly came to the fore, and almost at once there were references to Barry Lutze and to a local gang of cloud-runners known as the Hawks. As before, Hasson was disturbed to hear a note of uncritical admiration manifest itself in Theo's voice.

"I'll bet you," he said, deciding to risk endangering his newfound relationship with the boy, "the leader of that outfit is called Black Hawk."

Theo looked surprised. "How did you know?"

"It had to be that or Red Hawk. Those characters always have to hide behind some kind of label and it's amazing how limited their imaginations are. Practically every town I've ever been in has had a Black Hawk or a Red Eagle fluttering around the place at night terrorising the smaller kids, and the funny part of it is that each and every one of them thinks he's something special."

Theo stood up, carried his empty cereal dish to the recycler and returned to the table before speaking. "Anybody who wants to do any real flying has to cover up his name."

"That's not the impression I get from the sports pages and TV. Some people become rich and famous through real flying." Hasson knew from the expression on Theo's face that his words were having no effect. The phrase "real flying", as used by youngsters, meant flying illegally and dangerously, throwing off all petty restrictions and flying solely by instinct, flying without lights at night, playing aerial Catch-me-if-you-can in the canyons of city buildings. The inevitable consequence of that kind of "real flying" was a steady rain of broken bodies drifting to the ground as their power packs faded, but it was a characteristic of youth that it felt itself to be immune from calamity. Accidents always happened to somebody else.

One of the difficulties Hasson had encountered in his years of police work was that all the arguments were emotional rather than intellectual. He had lost count of the occasions on which he had interviewed members of a group who had just seen one of their number smeared along the side of a building or sliced in two on a concrete pylon. In every case there had been an undercurrent of feeling, akin to dawn-time superstition and primitive magical beliefs, that the deceased had brought misfortune down on himself by violating the group's code of behaviour in some way. He had defied the leader's authority, or had betrayed a friend, or had shown he was losing his nerve.

The death was never attributed to the fact that the young flier had been breaking the law—because that would have opened the door to the notion that controls were necessary. The nocturnal rogue flier, the dark Icarus, was the folk hero of the age. At those times Hasson had begun to wonder if the whole concept of policing, of being responsible for others, was no longer valid. The CG harness, as well as inspiring its wearer to flout authority, aided and abetted by giving him anonymity and superb mobility. A Black Hawk and his aerial cohort could range over thousands of square kilometres in the course of a single night and then disappear without trace, like a single raindrop falling into the ocean of society. In almost every case, the only way to bring a rogue flier to book was to go after him and physically hunt him down through the sky, an activity which was both difficult and dangerous, and it seemed that the number of hunters would always be pitifully inadequate. And when he was faced with a sky-struck youngster like Theo, automatically predisposed to worship the wrong kind of hero, it seemed to Hasson that he wasted his entire life.

". . . thinks nothing of boosting up to six or seven thousand metres and staying there for hours," Theo was saying. "Just think of it—seven kilometres straight up into the sky and thinks nothing of it."

Hasson had lost track of the subject, but he guessed it was Barry Lutze. "He must think something of it," he said, "otherwise he wouldn't have bothered to tell you about it."

"Why shouldn't he? It's more than . . ." Theo paused, obviously reframing a sentence. "It's more than anybody around here has done."

Hasson thought about his own brief sojourn on the edge of space, thirty kilometres up, but felt no desire to speak of it. "Doesn't he think it's a bit juvenile to go around calling himself Black Hawk?"

"Who said Barry is Black Hawk?"

"Have you got *two* top fliers around here? Barry Lutze and the mysterious Black Hawk? Do they never run across each other?"

"How would I know?" Theo demanded with a betrayed expression on his face as he felt for the coffee pot.

Hasson forebore to assist him, knowing that in the boy's eyes he was guilty of prying into things an adult could never understand. For the first time in history young people could escape the surveillance of their elders, and that was a prize which was never to be relinquished. Complete personal mobility had shrunk the world, and enormously widened the generation gap. Barrie had been brilliantly prescient in his understanding of the fact that there could be no communication between Peter Pan and any member of the grown-up world.

Hasson maintained a contrite silence while Theo, aided only by memory and the thin ray from a sensor ring on his right hand, located a cup and poured himself some coffee. He was wondering how best to open peace negotiations when Al Werry entered the kitchen from the rear of the house in a flurry of cold air. Werry was breathing deeply, apparently as a result of his snow-clearing activities. Hasson was slightly taken aback to see that he had kept his uniform on while performing the household chore, but he forgot about the idiosyncrasy when he noticed that Werry was looking strangely flustered.

"Go upstairs, Theo," he said without preamble. "Some people are coming to talk business."

Theo tilted his head enquiringly. "Can't I finish my . . .?"

"Upstairs," Werry snapped. "Move it."

"I'm going." Theo was reaching for his sensor cane, which was propped against the table, when there was the sound of the house's front door being thrown open, followed by heavy footsteps in the hall. A moment later the kitchen door opened and Buck Morlacher and Starr Pridgeon came into the room. Both were wearing flying suits and harnesses which bulked out their figures and made their presence in the domestic environment seem alien and hostile. Red patches glowed like warning pennants on Morlacher's slabby cheeks as he advanced on Werry, while behind him Pridgeon examined the contents of the room with an amused, semi-proprietary interest. Hasson felt a mixture of outrage, sadness and panic.

"I want to talk to you," Morlacher said to Werry, tapping him forcefully on the chest with a gloved finger. "In here." He nodded towards the front room and strode into it without turning to see if Werry was following. Werry, after one stricken glance at his son, followed him, leaving Pridgeon behind in the kitchen with Hasson and Theo.

"You know why I'm here," Morlacher's voice was thick with anger, filling both rooms.

Werry, in contrast, was almost inaudible. "If it's about that AC yesterday, Buck, I don't want you to think . . ."

"One of the reasons I'm here is that you're never in your Goddamn office where you're supposed to be, and the other one is about that murder on the east approach yesterday. It wasn't an AC, as you put it—it was a Goddamn murder, and I want to know what you've done about it."

"There isn't much more we can do," Werry said placatingly.

"*Isn't much more we can do,*" Morlacher mimicked. "A VIP comes to this city on business and gets murdered by some crazy shit-head punk, and there isn't much more we can do!"

Hasson, driven by the expression on Theo's face, stood up with the intention of closing the interconnecting door. He turned without having made sufficient preparation for the move, and froze as his back locked with a sensation like a glass dagger having been thrust between his vertebrae. He leaned on the table for a second, then carefully extended his hand to the door knob.

"Now, Buck, he wasn't really a VIP," Werry said in the other room.

"When I say the son-of-a-bitch was a VIP," Morlacher ground out, "that means the son-of-a-bitch was a VIP. He came up here to . . ."

Hasson slammed the door shut, reducing the overheard exchanges to a background rumble, and did his best to stand up straight. Pridgeon, who was walking around the room picking up small objects and replacing them, watched him with a kind of amiable contempt.

"Boy, you're really in a mess, Al's cousin from England," he said, smiling through the wisps of his moustache. His teeth had the almost-greenish tinge that comes from a permanent accumulation of food residue, and there were charcoal-coloured pockets of decay close to the gums between the incisors. "Car smash, wasn't it?"

"That's right." Hasson fought to keep back a conciliatory smile.

Pridgeon shook his head and hissed in his breath. "Shouldn't have been fruiting about in a car, Al's cousin from England. You shoulda been treading sky like a full-grown man. Look at young Theo! Theo's going to show 'em something as soon as he's able. That right, Theo?"

Theo Werry tightened his lips, disdaining to speak.

"Theo was on his way up to his room," Hasson said. "I think he had finished breakfast."

"Bull! He hasn't touched his coffee. Drink your coffee, Theo." Pridgeon winked at Hasson, pressed one finger to his lips in a silencing gesture and poured a thick stream of sugar from the stainless steel dispenser into the boy's cup. He stirred the resultant sludge and guided the cup into Theo's hand. Theo, his face alert and suspicious, gripped the cup but did not raise it to his mouth.

"I think you put in too much sugar," Hasson said lightly, sickened by his own complaisance. "We don't want Theo to get fat."

The playfulness disappeared from Pridgeon's face on the instant. He performed his intimidatory trick of abruptly fixing Hasson with a frowning, baleful voodoo stare, then came towards him, head thrust forward, moving silently on the balls of his feet. *This can't be happening to me,* Hasson thought, as he found himself nodding, smiling, shrugging, backing out of the kitchen, unable to bear the idea of the other man entering his personal space. Still under Pridgeon's threatening gaze, he reached the foot of the stairs and put his hand on the banister.

"Excuse me," he said, listening in fascinated dread to hear what words his mouth would utter next. "Nature calls."

He went up the stairs with the intention of going to his bedroom and locking himself inside, but the bathroom door was directly ahead and—spurred on by the notion of trying to make it appear that he really had needed to relieve himself—he went through it and thumbed the concave button on the handle. The silence in the bathroom beat inwards upon him.

"Nature calls," he breathed. "Oh, God! Nature calls!" Pressing the back of a hand to his lips to prevent their trembling, he sat down on a white-painted cane chair, remembering with a keen sense of loss the treasure trove of green-and-gold Serenix capsules he had so blithely thrown away. *I'll see a doctor and get some more,* he thought. *I'll get some more Sunday morning pills, and I'll get some television cassettes, and I'll be all right.* He lowered his head into his hands, feeling much as he had done while suspended in the high purple archways of the stratosphere—cold, remote, abandoned—and entered a period of timelessness.

His numb reverie ended with the sound of a door opening downstairs and a corresponding increase in the relentless, pounding surf-noise of Morlacher's anger. He waited a few seconds and opened the door just enough to give him a vertically slitted view down into the hall. Morlacher and Pridgeon were standing in it, occupying most of the floor space while they closed up their suits in preparation for flight. The door to the downstairs front room was closed and there was no sign of Al Werry. Pridgeon opened the entrance door, admitting a white blaze of snow-reflected daylight, and went outside. Morlacher was on the point of following him when there was an extra movement and a darkening of the trapezium of brilliance on the hall floor, and May Carpenter came into the house. She was carrying a net shopping bag and was dressed in a traditionally-styled tweed jacket and skirt trimmed with fur which gave her an oddly demure quality. Morlacher looked down at her with evident appreciation.

"May Carpenter," he said, putting on a rakish grin which was totally unlike any expression Hasson had seen him use previously, "you get prettier every time I see you. How do you do it?"

"Clean living, I guess," May replied, smiling, apparently unperturbed by his standing so close to her in the confines of the hall.

"That's one for the book," Morlacher chuckled. "All flower arranging and rug tying down at the PTA, is it?"

"Don't forget the cake competitions—you should see what I can do with a piping bag."

Morlacher laughed aloud, put his hands on May's waist and lowered his voice. "Seriously, May—why haven't you been over to see me since you got back into town?"

She squared her shoulders. "I've been busy. Besides, it isn't a girl's place to go calling on a man, is it? What would people say?"

Morlacher glanced towards the room where he had been talking to Al Werry, then drew May closer to him and kissed her. She relaxed into it for a moment and Hasson saw the slight grinding movement of her hips which had thrown every organic switch in his body the night before. He remained transfixed at his vantage point, terrified of being caught spying and yet completely unable to move away.

"I have to go now," Morlacher said as they separated. "I've got urgent business in town."

May looked up at him through quivering eyelashes. "Perhaps it's just as well."

"I'll call you," Morlacher whispered. "We'll fix something up." He turned and disappeared into the white radiance of the outside world. May watched him depart, closed the entrance door and—without pausing to remove her outdoor jacket—came straight up the stairs towards the bathroom, taking the steps two at a time. Hasson almost slammed the door shut before realising the action was bound to be noticed. Dry-mouthed and sick with apprehension, he whirled away from the door and stooped over the washbasin as though busy cleaning his hands. May passed the bathroom and went into a bedroom further along the landing.

Hasson, moving with the exaggerated stealth of a burglar in a stage production, left the bathroom and plunged into his own sanctuary, silently locking the door behind him. The discovery that his heart was labouring like a museum-piece engine strengthened his resolve to stay in his room as much as possible and avoid direct contact with the rest of humanity. He sat on the edge of the bed, turned on his television set and tried to become part of its miniaturised and manageable world.

He had been alone for some thirty minutes when there was a knock on the bedroom door, and on answering it he found Al Werry waiting on the landing. Werry had left off his uniform in favour of duracord slacks and a black sweater, and the change had made him look younger.

"Have you got a minute, Rob?" he said in a conspiratorial undertone. "I'd like to have a word with you."

Hasson opened the door fully and gestured for Werry to enter. "What's it about?"

"Can't you guess?"

Hasson avoided the other man's gaze. "I'm just passing through this neck of the woods, Al. There's no need to . . ."

"I know, but it would help me if I could talk to somebody. How about stepping out for a couple of beers?"

Hasson glanced at his television set which, once again because of time zone differences, was failing to provide the sort of programmes he wanted. "Would the television shops, stores, be open? I need to buy some cassettes."

"We can do that as well—no problem. What do you say to a beer?"

"I'm as dry as hell after last night," Hasson confessed, reaching for his topcoat. Werry slapped him on the shoulder with something like his normal bonhomie and led the way down the stairs, jigging noisily on his heels. A minute later they were in the police cruiser and swishing along a street whose wet black pavement gave it the appearance of a canal cut through a field of snow. As the car picked up speed thick chunks of snow which had encrusted its hood broke off in the slipstream and shattered on the windshield without making a sound. Hasson deduced that the snow was powder dry and light, unlike the variety he was familiar with in England. The car swung out on to the main road and topped a low rise, giving him a panoramic view of the city looking arctic-pure and idyllic in the generous sunlight. Colours had intensified in contrast to the pervasive whiteness and the windows of houses appeared as jet-black rectangles. Off to the south the fantastic pylon of the Chinook Hotel shone like a steel pin which was holding earth and sky together.

Hasson, already becoming familiar with the general layout of Tripletree, studied the aerial sculptures of the traffic control system and used them as a guide to pick out other landmarks. Among the latter, jutting up from a conglomerate of lesser buildings, was the glassy brown bulk of the furniture store where Theo had guided him on to the ring road the previous afternoon. On its roof, and glowing powerfully in spite of competition from the sun, was a huge bilaser projection representing a four-poster bed. Hasson frowned as an amber star began to wink on the computer panel of his memory.

"Quite a sign, that," he said, indicating the building to Werry. "Yesterday it was an armchair."

Werry grinned. "That's old Manny Weisner's latest toy. He changes the image two or three times a week, just for fun."

"He hasn't had it long then?"

"About three months or so." Werry turned his head and regarded Hasson with some curiosity. "Why do you ask?"

"No reason," Hasson said, trying to extinguish the amber star. Yesterday the sign had portrayed an armchair, and Theo Werry—who was blind—had said that it portrayed an armchair. The obvious explanation was that somebody had described the sign to him on a previous occasion when the image was the same and had not told him about the owner's habit of switching it around. Armchairs were one of the most common sale items in any furniture store, therefore the degree of coincidence involved in Theo's being right was not very great. Hasson dismissed the matter from his mind, irritated with its lingering habit of seizing on small shards of information and trying to build mosaic pictures with them. The question of what Werry wanted to talk to him about was of more immediate interest and importance. He hoped there were to be no confessions of corruption. In the past he had known other police officers to become too closely connected with men like Buck Morlacher, and none of the stories had happy endings. The thought of Morlacher brought back an associated memory of his own humiliating encounter with Starr Pridgeon, and it occurred to him that Morlacher and Pridgeon were a strangely assorted pair. He broached the subject to Werry.

"Fine example of an habitual criminal who has never done any time," Werry said. "Starr's been mixed up in everything from statutory rape to aggravated assault, but there was always a technical flaw in the police case against him. That or epidemic amnesia among the witnesses. He has a repair business over in Georgetown—washing machines, fridges, things like that—but he spends most of his time hanging around with Buck."

"What does Morlacher get out of it?"

"Company, I guess. Buck's got a real hair-trigger temper, specially when he's had a few belts, and he's got a habit of delicately hinting at his displeasure by kicking people in the crotch. If you see anybody walking around Tripletree with bow legs it doesn't mean they're cowhands—they used to work for Buck, that's all. Most folks find reasons to stay out of his way as much as they can, but Starr gets on pretty well with him."

Hasson nodded, mildly intrigued by Werry's steadfast practice of referring to everybody, even men he had reason to hate or despise, by their first names. He gave the impression of regarding all human failings, from the trivial to the most serious, with the same kind of careless tolerance, and it was a characteristic which Hasson found difficult to square with the profession of law enforcement. He sat quietly, coping with minor aches in his back and hip, until Werry brought the car to a halt outside a bar near the centre of Tripletree's shopping area.

"Ben's Holotronics is just round the corner," Werry said. "You go off and get your cassettes and I'll set up a couple of halfs." He went into the brownish dimness of the bar, walking with the jaunty lightness of a boxer in peak condition. He gave no sign of having anything preying on his mind. Hasson watched him disappear and made his way along the block through fierce sprays of reflected sunlight. Shadows flitted across his path every few seconds as fliers drifted down from the sky and landed on the flat roofs of buildings all around. It was the standard arrangement in modern cities, because CG fields broke up when any massive object, such as a wall, intersected their lines of force. That was the reason there were no aircraft powered by counter-gravity engines, and it was also the reason for modern public buildings having flat roofs or being surrounded by wide landing strips. Any flier who went too close to a wall found himself to be a flier no longer, but an ordinary mortal, fragile and afraid, hurtling towards the ground at an acceleration of close on a thousand centimetres per second squared. The same effect occurred when two CG fields interfered with each other, which was the reason for Air Police Sergeant Robert Hasson taking the big drop over the Birmingham Control Zone, the endless screaming drop which had almost . . .

Wrenching his thoughts back into the present, Hasson located the store where he had bought his television set and went inside. The owner, Ben, greeted him warily, but brightened up on learning that he had not returned with a complaint. It transpired that he had a good selection of six-hour programme cassettes and was able to supply Hasson with a number of complete runs of British comedy and musical shows, some of which had been recorded only the previous year.

Hasson, like an alcoholic contemplating a well-stocked cupboard, felt a comforting glow within himself as he left the store carrying a bulging plastic bag. He was now self-reliant, self-sufficient, equipped to live his own life. The evocative scent of dried hops and malt reached his nostrils and an impulse made him glance curiously into the window of the next store along the block. The proprietor, the oddly named Oliver Fan, had been an interesting and sympathetic character with an unusual line of sales talk. *You are not at ease within yourself.* That part was certainly true, Hasson mused. As a snap diagnosis it had been a hundred per cent accurate, but perhaps it was one of those all-purpose pieces of patter, such as used by fake fortune-tellers, designed to make the general sound like the particular. Perhaps it applied equally well to everybody who ever strayed through Oliver's door. *Believe me, I can help.* Would a charlatan say that? Would he not be inclined to use a more ambiguous form of words which would give him latitude for twisting and turning under legal scrutiny? Hasson hesitated for a long moment and then, filled with a curious timidity, went into the health food store.

"Good morning, Mr. Haldane," Oliver said from his position behind the glass counter. "It is good to see you again."

"Thank you." Hasson looked uncertainly around the laden shelves, breathed the mixture of heady aromas and felt lost for words, as though he had come to ask for a love philtre. "I . . . I wonder if . . ."

"Yes, I meant what I said—I can help you." Oliver gave Hasson a knowing, compassionate smile as he slid off his stool and moved along the counter. He was small and middle-aged—of exactly the same size, build and coloration as millions of other Asians—and yet he had an individuality which impressed Hasson as being as durable as the bedrock of China itself. His eyes, by contrast, were as homely, accessible and humorous as Laurel and Hardy or Mark Twain.

"That's a fairly sweeping statement," Hasson said, testing his ground.

"Is it? Then let's put it to the test." Oliver took a pair of iodine-tinted glasses from his breast pocket and put them on. "I already know you've been seriously hurt in a driving accident, and you probably know that I know, so we can take all that as given. There's no question of my using special powers or being able to see your aura the way some of those alternative medicine freaks claim to do. But—simply by looking at the way you walk and stand—I can tell that your back is giving you considerable pain. I would say that you also smashed up your left knee in the accident, but that it is fairly well on the mend and that it's your back that's causing all the trouble. Am I right?"

Hasson nodded, refusing to be impressed.

"So far so good—but there's more to it than that, isn't there? The physical injuries were bad, the spell in hospital was bad, the convalescence is long and painful and boring—but there was a time when you would have taken all that in your stride. Now you can't. You feel you're not the man you used to be. Am I right?"

"You're bound to be right," Hasson countered. "Is anybody the man he used to be? Are you?"

"Too general, eh? Too woolly? All right, you know your specific symptoms better than anybody, but I'll go over some of them for you. There's the depressions, the irrational fears, the inability to concentrate on simple things like reading, the poor memory, the pessimism about the future, the dozing like a lizard during the day followed by the inability to sleep properly at night unless you've had pills or booze. Am I right?"

"Well . . ."

"Is it difficult for you to meet strangers? Is it difficult for you to talk to me now?" Oliver took off his glasses as though to make confession easier, dismantling barriers.

Hasson wavered, torn between a cautious reserve and the urge to unburden himself to the stranger who seemed as though he could be more of a friend than any friend. "Supposing all those things were true, what could you do about it?"

Oliver appeared to relax a little. "The first thing to realise is that you and your body are a unity. You are one. There's no such thing as a physical injury that doesn't affect the mind, and there's no such thing as a mental injury that doesn't affect the body. If both aren't right, both are wrong."

Hasson felt a pang of disappointment—he had heard similar things from Dr. Colebrook and a series of therapists, none of whom seemed to realise that he had lost the ability to deal in abstracts, that words which did not have a clear-cut, one-to-one correspondence with concrete realities were completely meaningless to him.

"What does it all boil down to?" he said. "You said you could help. What can you do to stop my mind feeling pains in my back?"

Oliver sighed and gave him a look of rueful apology. "I'm sorry, Mr. Haldane—it looks as though I may have blown this one. I think I've let you down by saying the wrong things."

"So there's nothing you can do."

"I can give you these." Oliver took two cartons—one small and inscribed with Chinese characters in gold on a red background, the other large and plain—from the shelves behind him and placed them on the glass counter.

This is what it had to come down to, Hasson thought, his disillusionment complete. *Doctor Dobson's Famous Herbal Remedy And Spleen Rejuvenator.* "What are they?"

"Ginseng root and ordinary brewer's yeast in powder form."

"I see." Hasson paused, wondering if he should buy the products just to compensate Oliver for his time, then he shook his head and moved to the door. "Look, perhaps I'll come back another time. I'm keeping somebody waiting." He opened the door and began to hurry out of the store.

"Mr. Haldane!" Oliver's voice was urgent, but again there was no hint of annoyance over the loss of a sale.

Hasson looked back at him. "Yes?"

"How are your mouth ulcers today?"

"They hurt," Hasson replied, sensing with amazement that Oliver had deliberately and clinically taken some kind of action on his behalf, had chosen words that were tied to an objective reality for no reason other than his need to hear them. "How did you know?"

"I may go in for mystery and inscrutability, after all." Oliver gave him a wry smile. "It seems to get the best results."

Hasson closed the door and retraced his steps to the counter. "How did you know I have mouth ulcers?"

"Old Oriental trade secret, Mr. Haldane. The important thing is—would you like to get rid of them?"

"What would I have to do?" Hasson said.

Oliver handed him the two cartons he had left on the counter. "Just forget all those things I said about the unity of mind and body. This stuff, especially the yeast, will cure your mouth ulcers in a couple of days, and if you keep on taking it as directed you'll never be troubled that way again. That's something, isn't it?"

"It would be. How much do I owe you?"

"Try the stuff out first, make sure it works. You can call back and pay for it any time."

"Thanks." Hasson gazed thoughtfully at the storekeeper for a moment. "I really would like to know how you knew about the ulcers."

Oliver sighed, amiably exasperated. "Hospitals never learn. Even in this age, they never learn. They flood patients' bodies with broad-spectrum antibiotics and wipe out the intestinal bacteria which produce B-vitamins. A common symptom of B-vitamin deficiency is the appearance of mouth disorders, like those painful little ulcers, so what did the hospitals do? Would you believe that some of them are still painting them with potassium permanganate? It's completely ineffective, of course. They send people out looking like they've been swigging the blushful Hippocrene—you know, with purple-stained mouth—hardly able to eat, hardly able to digest what they do eat. Lacking in energy. Depressed. That's another symptom of B-vitamin deficiency, you know, and I'm getting back on to the kind of patter which nearly made you walk out of here in the first place."

"No, I'm interested." Hasson spent a few more minutes talking to Oliver about the relationship between diet and health, impressed and oddly comforted by his evangelistic fervour, then began to think about Al Werry waiting alone in the bar. He put his new purchases into the plastic bag on top of the TV cassettes and left the store after promising Oliver he would return early in the following week. In the bar he found Werry sitting in a corner booth with two full beer glasses and several empties on the table in front of him.

"I like drinking at lunchtime," Werry said. "It has four times the effect." His voice was slightly blurred and it dawned on Hasson that he had been personally responsible for emptying the half-litre glasses in a remarkably short time.

"You save money that way." Hasson drank from the glass which Werry pushed over to him. The lager it contained did not impress him as a beer, but he was grateful for its cleansing and tingling coolness. He eyed Werry over the rim of his glass, wondering what he wanted to talk about and hoping that no marked response would be required on his part. It seemed that every conversational exchange he had made since arriving in Tripletree had added to his burden of stresses, and it was a process which could not go on indefinitely, or even for much longer.

Werry took a long drink of beer and leaned forward with a solemn expression on his face. "Rob," he said, his voice charged with sincerity, "I really envy you."

"Is it my money or my looks?" Hasson parried, genuinely surprised.

"I'm not kidding, Rob. I envy you because you're a human being."

Hasson produced a lop-sided smile. "And you aren't?"

"That's exactly it." Werry was speaking with the utmost conviction, like a preacher trying to make a convert. "I'm not a human being."

Hasson, although baffled, realised with a sinking feeling that his tête-à-tête with Werry was not going to be an easy run. "Al, you'd pass for a human being any day."

"But that's all I do—I *pass* for a human being."

"Rhetorically speaking," Hasson said, wishing that Werry would get on with making his point in a more direct manner.

Werry shook his head. "It might be rhetoric, and it might not. Is it right to regard yourself as human if you haven't got any human feelings? Isn't that what the word human means—having humanity?"

"I'm sorry, Al." Hasson decided to show some impatience. "I haven't the slightest idea what you're talking about. What's the problem?"

Werry drank more beer, his eyes remaining fixed on Hasson's, somehow transferring a weight of responsibility to him. "You saw what happened at my place this morning. Buck came walking in like he owned the place and started leaning on me in front of my kid—and I just stood there and took it. What would you have done, Rob? What would you have done if you'd been in my shoes?"

"It's hard to say," Hasson replied, toying with his glass.

"All right—would you have got mad at him?"

"I daresay I would."

"That's it, you see. I didn't get mad—because there's something wrong with me. I don't feel anything. Sometimes I hear this little voice telling me I *ought* to get mad in a situation like that, but it doesn't carry any weight with me. I'm not afraid of Buck, but I don't care enough about anything to make it worth my while to stand up to him. Not even my own boy."

Hasson felt totally inadequate to receive such a confidence. "I don't think any of us are qualified to analyse ourselves the way you're trying to do, Al."

"There's no analysis—I'm just reporting certain facts," Werry said doggedly. "There's something wrong with me, something about the way I'm put together, and it affects everything I do, big or small. Tell the truth, Rob—when we met at the rail station yesterday you didn't know me from Adam, did you?"

"I haven't got much of a memory," Hasson said, feeling he had lost the thread of the discussion.

"It doesn't matter how good your memory is—the point is that you know what it's safe to forget. You know what you can let go. But I'm so busy trying to convince people I'm one of the boys that I remember everything that happens so that I can enthuse about it afterwards and tell everybody about the great times we had, but the truth is I never have any great times. I don't really exist, Rob."

Hasson began to feel embarrassed. "Listen, Al, do you think this is a . . .?"

"It's true," Werry cut in. "I don't really exist. I go around in my uniform most of the time, because when I'm wearing it I can convince myself I'm the city reeve. I haven't even got a sense of humour, Rob. I don't know what's funny and what isn't. All I do is remember things that other people laugh at, and then when I hear them again I laugh too, but when I hear a joke the first time I'm not even sure if it is a joke.

"I can't even argue with people, because as soon as I hear the other guy's point of view that becomes my point of view, as well. Then when I run into somebody who starts telling me the opposite I side with him right off.

"I don't even . . ." Werry paused to drink more beer, again fixing Hasson with an intent, brooding stare. "I don't even get much of a kick out of sex. I've read about the ecstasy of love, but I've never experienced it. When I'm on the job and it's right at the big moment . . . you know, when people are supposed to feel they're knocking on the door of paradise . . . all I can think about is that I might have left the lights on in my car, or that my backside is cold. Things like that."

Hasson felt a sudden heartless desire to laugh. He picked up his glass and studied the swarming of the tiny bubbles in the beer froth.

"That's part of the reason Sybil walked out on me," Werry continued. "We had arguments about the treatment for Theo's eyes—she wanted to let the hospital cut the middle out of them, and I wouldn't hear of it—but I think she got sick of living with somebody who was nobody. That's why I get on okay with May. She's another nobody. Her one ambition in life is to go around looking cute, and that's all she does, so I know where I am with her."

There was a longer pause, and Hasson knew that Werry had spoken his piece and that it was up to him to make some appropriate response. He glanced down at the plastic bag containing his dream cassettes and wished he could be locked in his bedroom in the parchment-coloured shade of drawn curtains, with the television set bestowing its sweet absolution. The unfairness of the situation—here was another person making impossible demands upon him—began to weigh heavily on his mind.

"Al," he said finally, "why are you telling me all this?"

Werry looked slightly nonplussed. "I thought you would want to know—after what you've seen at my place—but I've probably got it wrong."

"No, naturally I'd be concerned about a friend's problems—it's just that I've no idea of anything to say which might help."

Werry gave him a wan smile. "Who said I wanted help, Rob? I'd need to care about things being wrong before I could care about getting them put right." He finished his half-litre of beer and signalled a waiter at the other side of the room to bring a replacement.

Hasson gazed at him for a moment, then took refuge in a classical British non-sequitur. "Do you think there'll be any change in the weather?"

As soon as they got back to the house Hasson went up to his room and locked the door. The bed had been neatly made up and somebody had drawn back the curtains to admit the day's snow-reflected brilliance. He set his new purchases out on a tallboy, selected a cassette and dropped it into a slot on the television set. Gratifyingly familiar music seeped into the air and under the set's proscenium tiny figures began to act out a domestic comedy, part of a series he had watched in England only twelve months earlier. He drew the curtains together, shed his outer clothing and got into the bed, stoically waiting for the spasms in his back to subside. The artificial world of the television stage occupied his entire field of vision. It was as though he had retreated through time and space, back into his previous life, and he felt safe.

He had completed a day-and-a-half of rest and recuperation,

and the thought of three further months of the same kind of thing was unbearable. It was much better to lie curled up in a womb-cave of eider, and to submerge his mind in the dreaming of other men's dreams.

CHAPTER 6

CONTRARY TO HASSON'S fears and expectations, his new life in Tripletree quite abruptly became easy to bear.

One of the things which came to his rescue was a kind of variable time effect he had noticed previously when visiting a foreign country on leave. He had a theory that personal time was not measured by the clock, but by the number of fresh sensory impressions recorded by the mind. On the first day or two of a vacation, especially if the surroundings were very different to those of his daily norm, he continually experienced new sensations and those days seemed almost endless. The vacation felt as though it would go on for ever. Suddenly, however, the new environment became familiar, the number and frequency of surprise encounters with undiluted reality decreased, the mind returned to its customary complacency—and as soon as that state of consciousness was reached the remaining days of the holiday flickered by like slides on a speeded-up projector.

Hasson's theory had always depressed him a little because it both explained and confirmed the existence of a phenomenon described to him by his father—the acceleration of subjective time during later life. He had always sworn to himself that he would never get into a sense-numbing, mind-deadening rut, that he would never let the months and seasons and years slip through his fingers, but all at once he found the process working to his advantage. Time began to go faster, and the demands of each day grew less.

Keeping his promise to Oliver Fan, he began taking large spoonfuls of powdered brewer's yeast. At first he found the bitter, tongue-clogging substance almost impossible to swallow and had to swill it down with glasses of fruit juice. An immediate effect was that he became so bloated with internal gas production that he had difficulty in bending over, but Oliver had told him in advance that such a symptom would be proof of how much he needed the yeast's rich supply of B-vitamins. Placing his faith in Oliver's advice, he persevered with the yeast, rehearsing in his mind what he could remember from the impromptu lecture on its value as a source of anti-stress vitamins, biotin, cholin, folic acid, inositol, niacin, nucleic acid, pantothenic acid, iron, phosphorus and whole protein, as well as the complete B-vitamin complex. None of the biochemical terms had much meaning for Hasson, but two days after beginning the treatment he awoke to find that the mouth ulcers—which had plagued him for months—had vanished without trace. That benefit alone, he decided, was worth anything that Oliver was going to charge him.

He also began chewing tiny fragments of the ginseng root twice a day. It was a dark reddish-brown in colour, almost as tough as high-impact plastic, and tasted vaguely of grass. Hasson failed to see what good it could do him, but after his success with the mouth ulcers he was more than willing to give all of Oliver's recommendations a fair trial. His digestion improved, the gaseous pressure faded from his abdomen, his appetite returned, and in a short time he rediscovered a simple pleasure—that of looking forward to meals.

The food provided in the Werry household was not always to Hasson's taste, but in the middle of his second week there Ginny Carpenter—who had maintained her attitude of casual hostility towards him—departed on unspecified family business for a stay in Vancouver. May Carpenter did most of the cooking after that, and although she had her own set of culinary shortcomings these were more than compensated for in Hasson's view by the absence of her mother. It turned out that May had a part-time job in the office of a plant-hire company in Tripletree. She went to it four days a week, which meant that when Theo was at school Hasson had the house to himself, an arrangement which suited him perfectly.

He continued to spend as much time as possible watching television in his room, but in spite of his avowed wish to keep the shutters closed on the world he found himself thinking more and more about the real-life problems of his hosts. Al Werry, after his strange Saturday morning confessional in the downtown bar, reverted to his normal persona, going about his business with his suggestion of a swagger, looking fit and cheerful and competent, the picture of a well-adjusted career cop. He oversaw the activities of his minuscule force with a breezy carelessness which seemed not to have been affected by anything that had been said by Buck Morlacher.

Hasson was surprised to note that Morlacher—after having impinged on his life three times in rapid succession, each time looking more like a volcano on the point of eruption—had quieted down and virtually effaced himself from the scene. He wondered if Morlacher's change of attitude was simply due to the fact that the big man had other business interests and only got around to bedevilling Werry on occasion, or if it was something to do with May Carpenter. It was difficult for Hasson to be certain, but he had a feeling that the relationship between the two had developed since the encounter he had witnessed from the bathroom, and he became intrigued with the problem of determining what sort of person actually lived behind May's façade of primitive, uncomplicated sexuality.

According to Werry the façade was all there was. It was a judgment Hasson had thought to be unfair and insensitive, but as the days wore on he began to accept the fact that it was impossible to hold any kind of conversation with May. It began to appear to him that she was a gorgeous female android with only two modes of operation—signalling a romantic interest in the men she met, and actually indulging that interest. Hasson, perhaps by failing to make the correct responses, had confused the identification processes and caused himself to be placed in a category with which the mechanism was not programmed to deal. At times he felt guilty over thinking about another human being in such terms and decided that the failure in communications was due to his own real inadequacies, rather than those he imagined in May, but that insight—if insight it was—had no material effect on their relationship or lack of it. It appeared that she was prepared to deal with him only on her own terms and those terms were unacceptable to Hasson, partly out of consideration for Al Werry, partly because a remnant of pride would not allow him to stand in line with Buck Morlacher.

His relationship with Theo Werry became equally stagnant and unproductive, although in that case Hasson knew exactly what was wrong. The boy had all of the young male's natural respect for strength and courage, a respect which perhaps was enhanced by his handicap, and it was easy to guess the opinion he had formed of Hasson. In addition, the generation gap had been yawning between them ever since Hasson had put forward his views about angels in general, and their shared interests in music and literature were unable to bridge it.

Hasson chose to bide his time with Theo, watching closely for the first sign of encouragement, but the boy remained aloof, spending much of his free time in his bedroom. On a number of occasions as Hasson was going along the darkened landing he saw the door to Theo's room being limned with brief flashes of light, but he passed on his way each time, forcing himself to ignore the distress beacon, knowing that any attempt to answer it would be regarded as an intrusion. Once, well after midnight, he thought he heard a voice in the room and hesitated at the door, wondering if Theo could be having a nightmare. The sound died away almost immediately and Hasson passed on his way back to his television set, saddened by the idea that even the spurious vision of bad dreams could be cherished by a blind person.

As the new pattern of his life became a routine Hasson welcomed the dulling of his perceptions. Monotony was a mind-sapping drug to which he quickly became addicted and he drew comfort from a rapidly growing conviction that nothing of any significance would ever happen to him again, that night and day would continue to merge into the undemanding and featureless grey blur of eternity.

He was, therefore, taken by surprise by two miracles which occurred within a few days of each other.

The first miracle was external to Hasson and concerned the weather. For perhaps a week he was dimly aware of great changes taking place out of doors, of the light softening and the air growing warmer, of the sounds of trickling water replacing the night-time stillness. On the television there were reports of floods from other parts of the country, and once when Hasson looked out of his window he saw adults and children engaged in a British-style snowball fight in a nearby garden—an indication that the nature of the snow itself had changed. It had ceased being a light dry powder and now could be moulded into solidity, a mock-solidity which heralded its oncoming dissolution.

And then Hasson got up one morning to find that the long Albertan summer had begun.

Conditioned as he was to the protracted and uncertain seasons of the Western European seaboard, to the reluctant, ragged retreat of winter and the equally hesitant advance of milder weather, Hasson was scarcely able to comprehend what had happened. He was standing at his window looking out at a transformed world whose dominant colours were greens and yellows when he became aware of the fact that a second miracle had taken place.

There was no pain.

He had wakened and had risen from his bed without pain, accepting the condition as instinctively and unthinkingly as a creature of the wild stirring itself in response to the light of dawn. Hasson turned away from the window and looked down at himself, feeling the morning sunlight warm on his back, and made a few tentative movements like a gymnast limbering up for a display. There was no pain. He crossed to the bed, lay on it and got up again, proving to himself that he was a whole man. There was no pain. He touched his toes, then rotated his trunk so that he could touch the back of each heel with the opposite hand. There was no pain.

Hasson looked all around the bedroom, breathing deeply, the sudden possessor of untold riches, and made further discoveries. The room seemed more homely—its framed photographs nothing more than signs of family occupancy—but it had also grown too small. It was a suitable place for sleeping in at night, but there was a huge country outside, unexplored and intriguing, full of new places to visit, new sights to see, people to meet, food and drink to enjoy, fresh air to breathe . . .

With a rush of pleasure and gratitude, Hasson found he could contemplate the future without flinching, with no welling up of the darkness of the soul. He could anticipate reading, listening to music, swimming, attending parties, meeting girls, going to the theatre, perhaps even strapping on a CG harness and . . .

No!

The icy prickling on his forehead made Hasson realise he had gone too far. For a moment he had allowed himself to remember fully what it was like to stand on an invisible peak of nothingness, to look down at his booted feet and see them outlined clear and sharp against a background of fuzzy pastel geometries, to alter the focus of his eyes and translate that background into a dizzy, detailed spread of city blocks and squares many kilometres below, with rivers like twists of lead stapled by bridges, and ground cars shrunk to specks and halted by distance on white threads of concrete. He shook his head, dismissing the vision, and began to make plans whose scope did not extend beyond his own mortal capabilities.

Several days went by in which he was content to consolidate his new position, days in which he held himself ready to experience a mental and physical relapse. The bedroom which had once been a haven of security was mildly claustrophobic now. He reduced his time at the television set to an hour or two before going to bed, and instead began taking walks which were brief at first but which soon lasted three or more hours.

One of his first expeditions was to the health food store, where Oliver Fan gave him a single appraising glance and, without allowing him time to speak, said, "Good! Now that you've discovered some of the benefits of proper diet I can begin to make some real money out of you."

"Hold on," Hasson replied, feeling an ingenuous pleasure over the fact that his state of well-being was noticeable. "I admit I'm feeling better, but what makes you so sure your stuff had anything to do with it? How do I know I wasn't naturally on the point of picking up a little?"

"Do you believe that?"

"All I'm saying is that there must be a natural tendency to . . ."

"To get over illness and injury? There is. Homeostasis is the word for what you're talking about, Mr. Haldane. It's a powerful force, but we can assist it or hold it back—as in the case of those painful little moon craters in your mouth that you had for months and haven't got any more." Oliver shrugged expressively. "But if you feel you haven't had value for money . . ."

"I didn't mean that," Hasson said, reaching into his pocket.

Oliver grinned. "I know you didn't—you were just showing that you're no longer afraid of me."

"Afraid?"

"Yes. The day you first walked in here you were afraid of everybody in the world, including me. Please try to remember that, Mr. Haldane, because when you're making a journey it's very important to know where you started from."

"I remember it." Hasson stared at the little Asian for a moment, then on impulse extended his hand. Oliver shook hands with him in silence.

Hasson remained in the store for more than an hour, waiting in the background while other customers were being served, fascinated by Oliver's discourses on alternative medicine. At the end of the time he was still not entirely certain about Oliver's credentials and his fund of anecdotal case histories, but he was carrying a bag filled with new additions to his daily diet, the chief of which were live yoghurt and wheat germ. He also took with him the conviction that he had made a genuine friend, and in the days that followed he began calling regularly at the store, often just for the conversation. In spite of his professed commercialism, Oliver seemed happy enough with that arrangement and Hasson began to suspect that he himself was providing material for yet another dietetic dossier. He had no objections to that, and in fact had to fight off a fulfilling-of-the-prophecy syndrome which tempted him to give Oliver exaggerated reports of his progress.

The progress itself, however, was genuine and exhilarating. There were occasional psychological flat spots, reminders that elation was not a normal state of mind, but—as Dr. Colebrook had predicted for him—Hasson found he could handle them with increasing confidence and skill. He extended his programme of exercise to cover walks which lasted six or eight hours and took him many kilometres into the hilly terrain which lay to the north and west of the city. On those days he carried food he had prepared for himself, and during the lunch breaks would read and re-read an early copy of Leacock's *Literary Lapses* that he had found in a store in Tripletree.

He had bought the book with the intention of being prepared for a reconciliation with Theo, but the boy had kept up his barriers of reserve and Hasson had been too intent on his own affairs to try pressing the matter. In the process of recovery he became almost as obsessive and self-centred as he had been during the illness, pursuing fitness with a miserly lust, and in that state of mind the problems of others receded into unimportance. He knew, for example, that the return of warm weather had made the fantastic eyrie of the Chinook Hotel a much more habitable place at night, and that there had been a corresponding increase in the activities of the young fliers who used it as a headquarters. He was aware of Al Werry fretting about empathin parties in the tower, and the growing frequency of offences which air police jargon reduced to convenient sets of initials (AC, aerial collision; TDO, transportation of dense objects; AD, aerial defacation)—but which represented a genuine social menace—and none of it had any significance for him. He was isolated from the rest of humanity—just as surely as when hovering on the high threshold of space—fighting a private war, and had no reserves for anything else.

The closest he came to involvement was one morning when climbing a high saddleback to the west of the city, trying for a view of the Lesser Slave and Utikuma Lakes. A huge silence lay over the land, undisturbed by insects in that early part of the summer. There was no visible trace of human existence and it was possible to imagine that time moved at a slower pace here, that the last of the Pleistocene glaciers had barely retreated and the first of the Mongoliform tribes had yet to pick their way across the Bering Strait from the west.

Hasson had paused in his ascent and was trying to adjust his vision to accommodate the vast sloping perspectives when, without any warning, a brilliant source of light sprang into being in the sky to the north. The grass all around him glittered like tiny scimitars as if he had been caught in the beam of a powerful searchlight mounted on a helicopter, but the silence remained unbroken. Hasson shielded his eyes and tried to focus on the object, but it appeared as an anonymous centre of brilliance surrounded by a rosette of oily needles of light. The sky pulsed in blue circles.

As he watched, a second eye-searing point appeared close to the first, and that was followed by others until there was a ring of six miniature suns blazing down on Hasson, pinning him at the apex of a cone blinding radiance. The grass at his feet incandesced as though about to explode into flame.

Hasson experienced a moment of near-superstitious dread before ingrained mental disciplines came to his rescue. *Mirrors,* he thought. *A group of six fliers. Height anywhere from five hundred to a thousand metres—enough to render them invisible against a bright sky. Violations: TDO, for a start. Possible intended violations: Anything they feel like—there's nothing here to stop them.*

He lowered his gaze and resumed the climb, straining his ears for anything—a rush of air or the sound of voices—which might indicate that he was going to be caught up in something more serious than a juvenile game. The light continued to flicker around his path for a minute, then abruptly vanished. Hasson went on climbing for another minute before stopping and scanning the hemisphere of the sky. There was nothing out of the ordinary to be seen, but he no longer felt alone or remote from the 21st Century. The sky was a sentient blue lens.

A short time later, while he was seated on a rock having lunch, he was struck by a comforting thought which almost made him feel grateful to the group of unseen fliers. During the incident he had felt worried, tense, apprehensive—but not afraid. Not excessively so, anyway. There had been a certain coolness of the forehead and hollowness of the stomach, but none of the plethora of devastating symptoms he had come to know so well in recent months. There was a possibility that he was further along the road to recovery than he had realised.

He mused over the notion for a time, taking it to its logical conclusion, then rose to his feet and began walking in the direction of Tripletree.

"Sure thing! Borrow any harness you want—we've got lots of them just lying around the place." Werry gave Hasson an encouraging smile. "Do you want to use my spare suit?"

"No need—I won't be going up far." Hasson smiled in return, trying not to appear too diffident. "I'm just going to fool around for a while, really. See about getting acclimatised. You know how it is . . ."

"Can't say I do. I thought you were acrophobic."

"What made you think that?"

Werry shrugged. "Just an impression. It's nothing to be ashamed of, is it? Lots of people can't fly after a smash."

"That's true, but it doesn't apply in my case," Hasson said, wondering why he felt the need to lie.

"Well, do you want me to go up with you just to be sure?" Werry put aside the cloth he had been using to polish his boots and stood up, his uniform making him seem like an invader in the domesticity of his own kitchen. On returning from his walk Hasson had found him alone in the house and had decided to waste no time in setting up his private experiment.

"I can manage by myself," Hasson said, unable to keep the edge from his voice.

"Okay, Rob." Werry looked at him with a rueful expression. "I can't tell where helpfulness ends and nosiness begins. Sorry."

"No, I'm sorry. It's just that I'd feel self-conscious if . . ."

"This is what I was telling you about, Rob. This morning at the station Henry Corzyn—that's one of my patrolmen, the fat one—started griping about being short of money this month, and Victor—that's the kid—offered him a loan. Henry said he wasn't *that* hard up and didn't need to borrow money from anybody. And do you know what the kid did then?"

Hasson blinked. "Sighed with relief?"

"No. The kid took some bills out of his wallet and stuffed them into Henry's shirt pocket—and Henry let them stay there. After saying he wouldn't take a loan from anybody, he let the money stay in his pocket!"

"He must have wanted the loan, after all."

"That's what I'm getting at," Werry said with something like anguish in his eyes. "He must have wanted a loan, but he said he didn't—so how did the kid *know*? If that had been me I'd have believed Henry, and I'd have walked off and he'd probably have been calling me all kinds of bastard from now till Christmas. Or else I'd have got it wrong another way and forced money on him and hurt his feelings, and he'd still have ended up bad-mouthing me from now till Christmas. What I want to know is—how did young Victor know what was expected of him?"

"He's on an empathin kick," Hasson suggested.

"Not a chance! None of my . . ." Werry paused and gave Hasson a solemn stare. "I suppose that was a joke."

"Not much of a one," Hasson apologised. "Look, Al, you're not alone. Some people are naturally simpatico and the rest of us can only envy them. I'd like to be that way myself."

"I'm not envious—just puzzled." Werry sat down again and resumed polishing the already glossy toecap of a boot. "Would you like to go to a barbecue tonight?"

Hasson considered the idea and found it attractive. "That sounds good. I don't think I've ever been to a genuine barbecue."

"You'll enjoy this one. Buck's entertaining some visitors from out of town, so you can bet your life there'll be plenty of good food and good booze. He always lays it on thick."

Hasson did a mental double-take. "Are we talking about Buck Morlacher?"

"Yeah." Werry looked up at him with the calm innocence of a child. "Buck throws great parties, you know, and it's all right—I can bring as many guests as I want."

There's something wrong with one of us, Hasson thought incredulously. *Al, you're supposed to be the law around here.*

"May's going too," Werry said. "The three of us will shoot over to Buck's place around eight and drink the place dry. Okay?"

"I'll look forward to it." Hasson went out into the hall, selected a CG harness from the several that were hanging there, and checked its power unit. The familiar action evoked a stirring of unease, and the confidence he had felt earlier began to fade. It was possible, after all, that he was rushing his fences, making unreasonable demands on himself. He hesitated for a moment, then slung the harness over his shoulder and left the house. The sun was curving down towards the west, cubes of shadow filled the spaces between the houses and there was a touch of coolness in the air. Hasson estimated there were less than two hours of daylight left, but it was enough for his purpose.

It took him some forty minutes to reach a deserted area where old quarry works had permanently disfigured the ground to such an extent that it was unsuitable for any form of agriculture. An occasional flier could be seen overhead, speeding into or away from Tripletree, but he knew from experience that in such terrain he would be practically invisible to airborne travellers. He scanned the immediate surroundings, seeing everything with rich clarity in the coppery light, and began putting on the CG harness.

It was a standard model, with straps which felt too thin to Hasson's fingers. In normal flying there was no need for heavy webbing, because the counter-gravity field surrounded both the generator unit and the wearer, affecting them equally and creating no differential such as existed with a parachute or early troop-lifting jetpack. Police harnesses were much heavier and more positive in their connections, but for reasons which were unconnected with the laws of physics. The object was to ensure that no officer became separated from his CG unit during the aerial man-to-man combat which sometimes accompanied an arrest. Hasson was accustomed to heavy-duty straps and buckles, and although the benefit would have been purely psychological he would have preferred using police-style equipment for his crucial venture into the air.

He finished the flight preliminaries and, sensing that any further delay was inadvisable, rotated the master control on the belt panel to the primary position.

There was no perceptible effect. Hasson knew that was because the ground intersected the field in which he was now englobed, disrupting its onion-layer pattern of force lines. He also knew that he had only to perform a standing jump to make himself airborne, floating in geometrical equilibrium a short distance above the yellowed and dusty grass.

He bent his knees and raised his heels a little, making ready for the snapping release of muscular energy which was all that was needed to promote him from the status of man to that of a minor god. Seconds went by. Malicious, heart-pounding, blood-thundering seconds went by—and Hasson remained as much a part of the earth as any of the rocks which lay all about him. An audio alarm began a muted but steady chirping at his waist to remind him that power was being expended to no good effect. His thighs quivered from the effort of maintaining what should have been a transitory pose. And still he was unable to jump. Sweat prickled out on his forehead and cheeks; his stomach muscles clenched in nausea. And still he was unable to jump . . .

"To hell with it," he said, turning back the way he had come, and in that instant one part of his mind—representing the intolerant, unbending facet of Hasson's character, the side of him which regarded cowardice as the ultimate shame—took unilateral action. What he had intended to be an ordinary stride became an ungainly one-legged leap into the air, and he found himself drifting with nothing under his feet.

Sick, cheated and afraid, he reached for the master control, determined to kill the CG field. *Hold on,* came the silent shriek. *Don't waste the chance. You're off the ground now, and you're all right, and you can survive this. Make the best of it. Fly, man, FLY!*

Hasson was unable to believe what was happening to him as he touched the clinoselector, trading off a small fraction of lift to gain horizontal movement, and the ground began to flow underneath him. This was the moment. All he had to do now was advance the master control and he would go swooping up into the metallic sunlight, free of earth and all its petty restrictions, with new horizons unfurling on all sides and nothing above, around or below him but the pureness of wind-rivers . . .

NO! NO! NEVER!

He killed the CG field and slanted down into the tough grasses, stiff-limbed as a wooden mannikin. Green snares gripped his feet. He pitched forward and rolled over, crying aloud as pain lanced through his hip and lower back. The earth took hold of him and he clung to it, waiting for all sensations associated with flight to depart his body.

When he stood up a few minutes later he was able to move freely, and for that he felt grateful. He had learned a valuable lesson at the cost of only a brief period of mental distress and physical agony, and now that he knew for certain that his flying days were over he would be able to make reasonable and realistic plans for the long-term future.

As Hasson might have expected, Al Werry came downstairs prepared to go to the evening's barbecue in full reeve's uniform, complete with sidearm. Finding Hasson alone in the living room, he grinned ferociously and advanced on him crabwise, performing an elaborate shadow-boxing routine which ended with light pats on Hasson's cheeks.

"Where's May?" he whispered. "Have we time for a warmer before we go?"

Hasson nodded towards the kitchen. "She's in there with two boys who came round to stay with Theo."

"Then we do have time for a quick belt." Werry went to the sideboard and picked up a bottle. "Is rye okay? Have we educated your taste buds yet?"

"Rye's fine. With plenty of water."

"That's my boy." Werry made up two largish drinks and handed one to Hasson. "How did things go this afternoon? Did you do any cloud-running?"

Hasson sipped his drink before he spoke, realising that this was the crucial first moment of his new life. "Things went very badly. I did one short hop, and I hated it."

"That's only natural. It'll take a while for you to get used to going up again."

"No, it's more serious than that," Hasson said, keeping his voice level. "I'm finished flying. I won't *be* going up again."

"It's an overrated pastime, anyway," Werry said moodily, staring into his drink. "They'll give you a desk job, won't they?"

"I imagine so—acrophobia is a recognised occupational disease in the force."

The cheerful expression returned to Werry's face. "That's not so bad, then. Drink up and forget about it." He was following his own advice when May Carpenter emerged from the kitchen wearing gold boots, slacks and a quilted gold anorak. She looked at Werry and her jaw sagged.

"My God," she said, "you're not going dressed up like *that*!"

Werry looked down at himself. "What's wrong with the way I'm dressed?"

"What's wrong?" She glanced at Hasson, then turned back to Werry. "Al, is it a costume ball or are you planning to raid the joint?"

Werry made placating gestures with his free hand. "Honey, this isn't just a social occasion tonight. Buck has some very important visitors—least he thinks they're important—and he'll want them to see that he hobnobs with the city reeve."

May sighed, looking beautifully disconsolate. "Go into the kitchen and say goodnight to Theo."

"There's no need," Werry said. "He never notices whether I'm here or not. Let's go, folks—it's crazy to stay here drinking our own booze when we could be out drinking somebody else's. Isn't that right, Rob?"

Hasson set his glass down. "Your argument is economically sound."

"I'm ready," May said. "Are we flying or driving?"

"Driving." Werry opened the door to the hall and ushered May through it with exaggerated courtliness. "Didn't Rob tell you he's been grounded?"

"No," May said incuriously, walking towards the front door.

"It's true—I can't fly any more," Hasson said to her retreating back, putting in some practice at making the admission. She appeared not to notice. When they got into the waiting police cruiser Hasson sat alone in the rear seat, feeling lonely in the spacious darkness and wishing he had a woman with him. Almost any woman in the world would have been suitable, as long as she provided companionship. As the car slid silently along dim streets he stared nostalgically at the windows of the houses they passed—mellow, glowing rectangles, some of them framing tableaux of family life, the figures frozen in mid-gesture by the briefness of the glimpses he received. Hasson distracted himself by trying to invent characters and backgrounds for the waxwork people, but he could smell the light flowery perfume May was wearing and his thoughts kept coming back to her.

Weeks of discreet observation had given him no deeper insights into her personality, and he was still unable to see what had brought Werry and her together in the first place. As far as he could determine, Werry provided accommodation and food for May, and sometimes for her mother, and in return she gave some assistance with the running of the household. It was to be presumed that they had a sexual relationship, but there was an absence of any kind of mutual commitment which Hasson found baffling and disturbing.

Is this what life is like on the ground? he wondered. His instincts had led him to reject Werry's claim that he and May were non-people, merely realistic lay figures imitating the movements of life—but supposing the fantastic hypothesis were true? Insidious and shameful thoughts began to burgeon in Hasson's mind. Why not throw overboard all cumbersome precepts concerned with honour and truth? Why not consider the situation as a straightforward problem in logic or mathematics? X is a man restored to health and with an increasing need for a safety valve to release biological pressures. Y is a man who is incapable of feeling love, hate or jealousy. Z is a woman for whom the concept of fidelity has little meaning. The current relationship can be expressed as X + (YZ), but why not do a little algebraic manipulation, the sort of thing that is done all the time, and change it to Y + (XZ)?

Hasson gazed at May's silhouette, for the moment allowing himself to see her as a love machine, a human engine which would respond in a certain guaranteed way if he pressed the right buttons—then a rising tide of self-disgust obliterated all the symbols from his mind. Al Werry was a human being, not a mathematical abstraction, and if the things he said about himself were true it meant that he had gained very little from life, and for that reason should be protected rather than plundered. Equally, May was a human being and if she appeared two-dimensional to him the fault had to lie in his inability to perceive depth.

The car had been climbing a gentle hill on the western outskirts of Tripletree and now it swung on to a private road which tunnelled through banks of rhododendrons and other shrubs which Hasson was unable to name. After a few seconds of utter darkness it emerged on a flat summit where a rambling floodlit house presided over a glittering view of the city. Tripletree itself was a spilled hoard of jewellery, a central mound of every kind and colour of precious stone surrounded by outflung necklets of diamond and topaz. The aerial highways hung over it in pastel brilliance, each generously seeded with the lights of night-time fliers, and above them a few first magnitude stars pierced the canopy of radiance with their own patient lustre. Fairy lanterns had been lit on a patio at the side of the house, there was the sound of music and thronging figures surrounded a column of smoke from what appeared to be a huge charcoal grill.

"We must have come to the wrong place," Hasson said ironically.

"No, this is definitely Buck's house," Werry replied, bringing the car to a halt. "I ought to know my way around Tripletree by this time."

They got out of the car and walked towards the centre of activity with May patting her hair into place and Werry tugging various parts of his uniform into the required degree of smoothness. Hasson lagged a little behind them, experiencing the curious mixture of hesitancy and anticipation he always felt when arriving at a party which was well under way. He expected their entrance to go unnoticed, but the tall heavy-shouldered figure of Buck Morlacher came towards them immediately. An old-style striped apron was tied around his waist, he was carrying a long fork and the heat from the charcoal had inflamed the triangular patches of red on his cheeks. He went straight to May, affecting not to see Werry or Hasson, put an arm around her shoulders and whispered briefly into her blonde hair. May listened for a moment and began to laugh.

"Evening, Buck," Werry said pleasantly. "Looks like the party's going well. I brought Rob along to show him how we do these things in Alberta."

Morlacher looked at him with cold eyes, still not acknowledging Hasson's presence, and said, "The booze is over by the fountain."

Werry laughed. "That's all we need to know. Come on, Rob." He took Hasson's arm and began to guide him across the patio.

Hasson refused to move. "Perhaps May would like a drink."

"I can look after May," Morlacher said, tilting his head to give Hasson an appraising stare.

"You're busy with the cooking." Hasson addressed himself directly to May. "The usual, is it? Rye and ginger?"

"I . . ." She gazed back at him, wide-eyed and flustered. "I'm not thirsty yet."

Morlacher tightened his grip on her shoulders. "I'll fix the lady a drink when she's ready. What's the rush?"

Werry pulled harder on Hasson's arm. "That's right, Rob. It's every man for himself around here."

Morlacher nodded slowly and an unexpected look of satisfaction appeared on his face. "Talking about every man for himself, Reeve Werry, I did something today that you should have thought of a long time ago."

"Yeah?" Werry released Hasson's arm. "What was that?"

"You know that black hound of mine? The one I tried to shoot last year for tearing a piece out of Eddie Bennett's leg?"

"You put him down, did you?"

"No—I put him to work. Starr and I went out to the farm and netted him today and carried him up to the hotel and turned him loose up there. Any punks who move in tonight are going to move out a hell of a sight faster." Morlacher grinned, showing his inhumanly powerful teeth.

Werry looked impressed. "That should make a difference. I'll get one of my boys to drop him some food every day."

"No you won't—I want the brute to stay mean and hungry. From now on he's on a strict diet of angel food. Get it?"

"Hey, that's a good one," Werry said, chuckling. He turned and sauntered away across the patio, waving salaam-like greetings to people he recognised, giving the impression he had forgotten the existence of Hasson and May. Hasson, feeling betrayed, followed in his wake, noting as he did so that Morlacher and May were moving off in the direction of the house. He caught up with Werry at a portable bar where two men in white jackets were dispensing liquor in heavy goblets which were decorated with simulated rubies.

"Do me a favour," Werry said to Hasson as soon as they had obtained their drinks, "try not to upset Buck—it only makes life difficult for me. Why were you arguing with him, anyway?"

"That's a good question," Hasson said in a stony voice, "but I think I've forgotten the answer."

Werry looked perplexed. "I hope you're not going to start going funny on me, Rob. I'm off to do a bit of mingling. See you around." He moved away towards a group of men and women who were dancing in a corner of the patio.

Hasson stared after him in exasperation, then turned his thoughts to the question of what he was going to do during the next four or five hours. There appeared to be about thirty people in the general area. Many of them were dressed in duvet garments of one kind or another to ward off the early season coolness, with the result that the atmosphere of the gathering was an uneasy blend of party and heroic picnic. A number of the guests were wearing identical gold badges. Hasson spoke to a gaunt, shivering middle-aged man who was determinedly lowering drink after drink in the manner of one who wanted no memory of the occasion, and learned that the visitors were members of an association of chambers of commerce from the western States. They were on a goodwill tour of the Canadian federation and the gaunt man gave the impression of suffering deep regrets over having strayed so far north from his home in Pasadena.

Hasson remained with him for some time discussing the effects of latitude on climate. Other tourists joined in and when they heard Hasson's British accent the conversation developed into a lively debate on the effects of longitude on climate. Hasson, far from being bored, took pleasure in his newly-regained ability to mix and interact with strangers. He drank, obtained food from volunteer cooks at the grill, drank some more, danced with various women wearing gold badges, and smoked his first cigar in months.

In between times, he observed that Morlacher and May were absent from the rest of the assembly for the best part of an hour, but by then he had reached a condition of malty benevolence in which he was prepared to concede that May could have been looking at her host's stamp collection, and in which he saw clearly that other people's problems were no concern of his. Life on the ground, it seemed, could be perfectly acceptable as long as one was prepared to live and let live. The notion struck Hasson, retired air cop and reformed meddler, with all the force of a brand-new philosophical concept, and he was exploring its implications when the dance music was suddenly switched off and everybody near him turned to look at something which had begun to happen in the centre of the patio. He moved into a clear space to get a better view.

Buck Morlacher and two other men were wheeling a flat-bed bilaser projector into place. They locked its wheels, made some control adjustments and a glowing image of the Chinook Hotel sprang into being above the machine. The solid-seeming representation was about three metres high and showed the building as it might have appeared in the architect's mind, complete with scenic elevators and roof gardens. A murmur of appreciation was heard among the viewers.

"Sorry to interrupt your enjoyment, ladies and gentlemen—but I guess you knew there had to be a catch somewhere," Morlacher announced with a grin that hovered between candour and coyness. "Don't worry, though—this is only going to take up a minute of your time—and I think you'll agree it's worth that much to become acquainted with some of the truly wonderful amenities that Central Alberta can offer to businessmen who are interested in reaching new suppliers and new markets. Now I know the Western Prairies air corridor stops a few hundred kilometres south of here, but that's nothing but a minor detail when you think of the potential for new business that this area offers."

Morlacher produced a sheet of paper and began to read out statistics which supported his argument. Most of his audience appeared suitably interested, although there was a stealthy drift from the outskirts of the circle in the direction of the bar. Hasson discovered that his own goblet was empty. He turned to go for a replenishment, but stopped in mid-stride as a new sound impinged on his hearing.

It was an unexpected, alien, unidentifiable sound—a ghastly hybrid between a moan and a scream which immediately conjured unwanted thoughts of demons and banshees, and which brought a coldness to the heart. Morlacher stopped speaking as the sobbing wail swiftly reached a crescendo which beat on the gathering like a siren.

It's coming from above, Hasson thought, but before he could look upwards into the night sky there was a kind of pulpy explosion near the centre of the patio and a number of women shrieked with horror. Hasson shouldered his way forward and saw something black and incredibly bloody lying on the stone slabs.

For an instant he was unable to identify the grisly object—it could have been an insane and meaningless concoction of charnel house nightmares—then he realised he was looking at the flattened, ruptured body of a large black mastiff. Spatters of crimson reached out from it in all directions. From the condition of the dog's carcase Hasson estimated that it had been dropped from a height of several hundred metres.

That almost happened to me once, he thought bemusedly. *But now I'm safe. I don't care about that dog—because now I'm safe.*

"You lousy *bastards*!" Morlacher roared as he leaped on to the low platform of the bilaser projector. His clothing was disfigured by a diagonal streak of red blotches. He shook his fist at the sky and its unseen habitants, and his presence in the cone of laser rays caused the solid image of the Chinook Hotel to shimmer and dissolve like a vision projected on a screen of smoke.

"You lousy shit-head bastards!" Morlacher bellowed, his massive figure seeming to swell with uncontrollable fury. "I'll get you for this."

He lowered his gaze and, apparently remembering the presence of his out-of-town guests, made a visible effort to bring himself under control. A shocked silence had descended over the patio, a silence which was disturbed only by the faint sounds of a woman crying. Morlacher took out a handkerchief and dabbed himself with it while he muttered apologies to those nearest him. He stepped down off the platform and began to move through the hushed assembly, his eyes questing from side to side. Hasson guessed he was looking for Al Werry.

"Tough luck, Al," Hasson murmured to himself as he turned towards the bar with his empty goblet. "A policeman's lot is not a happy one."

CHAPTER 7

WRAPPED TIGHT IN a cocoon of self-interest, Hasson continued to live as quietly as he possibly could, devoting all his attention to his own welfare.

In that isolationist and myopic frame of mind, the importance he attached to events was reduced on a logarithmic scale by their distance from the core of his own being. News of world trade and shifts in global strategies, for example, had so little significance as scarcely to register on his consciousness. He was aware of Al Werry being unusually busy on the days following the barbecue, spending long hours rousting aerial vagabonds, but that too was at a remove from the hub of reality and no more worthy of his concern than the activities of the shadow people in a poor holoplay.

The truly momentous happenings in Hasson's life, the events which could stir his imagination and dominate his thoughts, were of a different class altogether: the discovery that his skin was becoming tanned as a result of his prolonged spells in the open air; his growing ability to jog for kilometres over terrain which formerly would have exhausted him at walking pace; the epicurean pleasures he had learned to derive from such noble arts as breathing properly and sleeping well. He made living an end in itself, a goal which was continuously achieved, and as the days progressed he felt increasingly safe, secure, impregnable . . .

A five-hour trek across rolling grasslands had left Hasson feeling hot, dusty and tired. He took a cool shower and changed into fresh clothing, then realised he had neglected to take his full quota of yeast for the day. Oliver Fan had promised him he would eventually learn to enjoy the taste of the aromatic brown powder, and although he had made little progress in that direction he conscientiously swallowed fifty grammes of it on a daily basis. He picked up the yeast carton and went downstairs, pausing for a moment in the crowded hall as he heard a familiar twanging voice coming from the direction of the kitchen. It appeared that Ginny Carpenter had returned from her stay in British Columbia.

When he went into the kitchen he saw Werry and May Carpenter seated at the round table with beer glasses in front of them, while Ginny—as spiky and sparkly as ever—was standing with her back to a counter, arms folded, relating details of her trip.

"Well, look who it is," she said. "The quiet limey."

"I'm very well, thank you," Hasson replied politely. "How are you?" He turned and nodded greetings to Werry and May, then took a glass out of a cupboard.

Ginny examined him critically, blinking a little, and spoke as if he was no longer present. "He's looking a bit more human, anyways —I told you all he needed was a spell of good food and good home cooking."

Hasson smiled at her. "Is that why you went away?"

Her face stiffened and she looked at Werry with scandalised eyes, seeking support.

"You needn't try to put one over on Rob these days," Werry said, looking delighted. "He's as sharp as a razor lately—it must be something to do with that blasting powder he keeps swallowing."

"What is that stuff?" Ginny watched suspiciously while Hasson took a spoonful of yeast and washed it down with water from the tap.

"Yeast. He gets it from the health food store on Second Street."

"Olly Fan's place?" Ginny gave a yelp of derision. "Anybody who goes in there needs his bumps felt."

"Mum!" May Carpenter whispered. "That's not a very nice thing to . . ."

Ginny waved her into silence. "You can't tell me anything about those Chinks. I see 'em hundreds of times in their corner stores. You know what they do to pass the time?"

"You've told us before," May said wearily, with a flickering glance at the ceiling.

"They keep opening matchboxes and taking one match out of each. Nobody's going to miss one match out of each, you see. Just standing there all the time—opening matchboxes and taking one match out of each. *We* wouldn't do a thing like that, but after they've done it fifty times they've made the price of an extra box of matches." Ginny paused, having completed her case, and looked at the others with a mixture of indignation and triumph. "What do you say to that?"

"What do they sell them in?" Hasson said, thinking about Oliver and his insight and compassion.

Ginny frowned. "What do you mean?"

"I mean what do they sell those extra matches in? According to you they've got fifty extra matches, but no box to sell them in." Hasson nodded to Werry. "Did anybody ever sell you a paper bag full of matches?"

"He's got you there," Werry shouted gleefully, gripping Ginny's thigh. "You never thought of that one."

"Just you listen to me, Al Werry, and I'll *tell* you what they do," she snapped, beating his hand away. She opened her mouth several times, as though prompting it to go ahead and produce an explanation by itself. Finally, when it had become obvious to her that no suitable words were forthcoming, she looked at Hasson with eyes which were dulled with hatred.

"I haven't got time to stand here jawing all night," she said. "I'm going to make the dinner."

The ultimate weapon, Hasson thought, but already he felt mildly disappointed in himself for having squared up to a tiny twig of a woman whose aggression was probably a sign of unhappiness.

"I shouldn't have made that crack about your cooking," he said, smiling. "I'll look forward to eating anything you want to conjure up for us."

"Have a beer, Rob," Werry put in. "I'm on duty tonight, so I won't be able to have one with you later." He stood up, took a can of beer from the refrigerator and led the way into the front room. Hasson winked at Ginny, changing her expression to one of bafflement, and went after Werry. The two men sat for an hour during most of which Werry talked about the difficulties of police work and how much better off he would be in some other occupation. He looked composed and dauntingly immaculate, but there was a new soberness in his eyes which suggested that Buck Morlacher had managed to penetrate his mental armour, and he spoke at length about his renewed efforts to block off the Chinook Hotel to trespassers. His two air patrolmen, Henry Corzyn and Victor Quigg, had been detailed to circle the lofty upper section from before dusk to prevent unauthorised entry. Werry himself had arranged to spell them in four-hour shifts during the night vigil, which was why he was to go on duty as soon as he had eaten dinner.

"The trouble is I've been extra busy during the day, as well," he grumbled, tapping the side of his beer glass to revive the head. "Now that the good flying weather is back, kids are drifting in from all over. The Chinook draws them like a magnet, you see. We keep turning them back or busting them for flight offences, but there's always another lot on the way and we can't stop them all. Especially after dark.

"Sometimes I feel like getting hold of a tonne of hidyne and blowing the stick out from under the big lolly. It just isn't rignt for most of the city's police force to be tied up trying to look after one man's private property."

"It's bound to become dangerous with neglect," Hasson said. "Maybe you could get an order to have it pulled down."

"Maybe, but it would take years." Werry gave an introspective sigh. "You can see the attraction it must have for some kids. They can have their own world up there—a world that no adults ever see. They can have their own kind of society up there, with different rules, and no parents butting in to spoil things. The parents can be two or three hundred kilometres away, or more, not even knowing where the kids are, and that's a bad thing, Rob."

"I know, but the only way you could hope to link social units together again, the way they were in pre-flight days, would be to implant radio tracers in everybody—and that sort of thing isn't on the cards."

"I don't know," Werry said moodily. "I think it'll come to that some day. I really do." He jumped to his feet and did his now-familiar parody of a military salute as May appeared in the doorway to announce that dinner was ready.

Hasson followed him into the kitchen and noted that the table had been set for four. "Where's Theo tonight?" he said, realising that he had done very little in the past few days to rebuild his relationship with the boy.

"He took some milk and cold cuts up to his room," May said. "He wants to listen to the radio in peace."

"Oh?" Hasson recalled an earlier conversation with Theo. "I didn't know he was keen on radio."

"He listens quite a lot at night," Werry said. "It's a big help to him, having the radio."

May nodded her agreement. "That's right—it means a lot to him."

Hasson sat down, thoughtfully stroking his chin, and turned his attention to the food his stomach so urgently craved. The main course was built around a spiced meat loaf which he found enjoyable, and he further disconcerted Ginny Carpenter by giving it lavish praise. Dessert was gin-flavoured ice cream with lychees, a combination he found slightly sickly, but he asked for a second helping and had developed a comfortable tightness around his middle by the time coffee was served.

"When somebody tells you to build yourself up you don't fool around," Werry commented jovially. "It seems to me . . ." He broke off and muttered with irritation as the police radio on his wrist emitted a shrill bleep. There was a moment of silence, during which he sat shaking his head, then the radio sounded again.

"Sorry, folks." Werry touched a button on the communicator and spoke into it. "Reeve Werry here. What's your problem?"

"Al, this is Henry Corzyn," the radio said in a thin, urgent voice. "I'm at the Chinook. You'd better get over here as fast as you can."

"Henry, I said I'd be there nine o'clock. Can't you wait till I . . .?"

"This won't wait, Al. There's been some kind of explosion on the bottom floor of the hotel section—and I think there's a fire starting."

"A fire?" Werry looked around the table with arched brows. "There's nothing to burn up there, is there?"

"The place is full of lumber and scaffolding and partitions, Al. The contractor just walked off and left the place *full* of stuff."

"Well, have you called the fire service?"

"Victor did that, but it isn't going to help. The hotel's four hundred metres up, and our hoses and sonics haven't a hope in hell of reaching that far."

"You're right! Know something, Henry? You're dead right!" Unexpectedly, a peaceful, beatific smile spread across Werry's features. "Do you think we stand any chance of saying goodbye to our local landmark?"

There was a pause before Corzyn spoke again, and this time his voice was curiously hesitant. "I don't know about that, Al—I only saw a bit of a flare-up and it might die down again, for all I know."

"We'll just have to hope for the best," Werry said.

"This is serious, Al," the radio came back. "It looks like some people have been hurt bad."

"People?" Werry sat up straight. "What in hell are you talking about? What people?"

"I told you there was an explosion, Al. Leastways, that's what it seemed like to me. Some kid got blown right out of an elevator shaft and he's hurt pretty bad."

"*Christ Almighty!*" Werry sprang to his feet, sending his chair tumbling behind him, snatched his tunic from another chair and ran to the door. Hasson saw May staring after him, both hands pressed to her mouth, then he too was out in the hall and running behind Werry. They burst out into the breezy, star-crowned darkness surrounding the house and sprinted for Werry's cruiser parked in the street.

Hasson paused at the car as an unnerving idea occurred to him. "Al, are you flying or driving?"

"I was going to fly." Werry glanced into the car where his harness lay on the rear seat. "Hell, by the time I get strapped up I could be three-quarter way to the Chinook. Jump in!"

Hasson slid into the front passenger seat and in a few seconds the car was broadsiding out on to the main road which ran towards the centre of Tripletree and the south side. As it plunged towards the massed lights and the whorls of glowing aerial highways Werry called up Corzyn on the car radio.

"I'm on my way, Henry," he said briskly. "Give me that again about somebody falling out of an elevator shaft. Is he dead?"

"He isn't dead, Al—broke up a bit and concussed. I've called an ambulance for him."

"But if he fell four hundred metres . . ."

"No, he was up there when the explosion happened—sounds like a bomb to me, Al—and as far as I can tell he got blasted into the elevator shaft and hit the wall. Lucky for him his CG unit was all right and he had enough savvy left to switch it on. He was floating down the wind like a soap bubble when Victor and me put a line on him and brought him down."

"Get an ID on him as soon as you can." Werry drummed his fingers on the steering wheel. "How did he get in there, anyway?"

There was a sputtering silence. "Well . . . Victor and me got cold up there and we didn't see any harm in calling in at Ronnie's place for a cup of something to warm us up. I guess he could have got in then."

"That's wonderful," Werry said. "That's really wonderful, Henry."

"Al, there's fourteen Goddamn floors in the Chinook and it's four or five hundred metres all round. Two of us flitting around in the dark can't seal up a place that big. There could be a whole Goddamn procession going in and out, for all we would know about it." Corzyn sounded hurt and aggrieved.

"All right, all right." Werry glanced at Hasson and pulled a face. "What's all this about a bomb?"

"That's what it seems like to me, Al. What else would cause an explosion? I found out there's a lot of paint stored on some of the floors, but that would only burn, wouldn't it? It wouldn't blow up."

"You could be right. Do you think the kid who got hurt was fooling around with explosives and blew himself up by accident?"

"He's out cold now, Al, but it doesn't look that way to me."

"What do you say, then?"

There was an even longer crackling pause. "Victor saw Buck Morlacher at the hotel this morning."

"Aw, *no*," Werry groaned, shaking his head. "Henry, don't say things like that over the air. In fact, don't say them at all. Hang on—I'll be there in a couple of minutes."

Werry accelerated past a group of slow-moving cars and the dark hulk of Weisner's furniture store came into view ahead. The bilaser projector on its roof had created a gigantic dining table which glowed against the night sky. The sight of it caused an uneasy stirring in Hasson's memory, but his thoughts were completely dominated by the conversation he had just heard. On the night of the barbecue Morlacher had seemed dangerously near his limit of control, and from what Hasson knew of the big man it seemed entirely possible that he would go as far as planting booby traps to clear his property of what he regarded as vermin.

"I don't like the sound of this, Rob," Werry said thoughtfully. "I don't like it one bit."

Hasson gave him a sympathetic glance. "You think Morlacher would have gone that far?"

"Buck thinks he can get away with anything."

"So what'll you do?"

"Who says I've got to do anything?" Werry demanded, hunching his shoulders like a man warding off blows. "We don't even know that Buck had anything to do with this. It seems to me that I've got to have some kind of proof before I think about arresting a man like Buck."

"Nobody's going to argue with you on that one," Hasson said, resolving not to raise the matter again. The flashing lights of an ambulance expanded out of the distance and momentarily washed the interior of the police car with ruddy brilliance as the two vehicles passed. The bleat of the ambulance's siren dopplered away into a low growl. Werry swung his car into the cross-street from which the ambulance had emerged and the Chinook Hotel came into view as a vertical thread of grey light surmounted by a vague smudge of weak radiance.

Hasson, who had been looking out for something spectacular, had to remind himself that the hotel building itself was four hundred metres above ground, that a person standing on its lowest floor could have looked down on the old Empire State Building. The fantastic structure, made feasible only by 21st century materials and engineering techniques, was a monument to one family's megalomania and arrogance. He could visualise, and almost condone, the poisonous rage which boiled through Morlacher's mind each time he looked at the edifice which had annihilated the parental fortune and which, instead of repaying the investment with profit and prestige, had made him the butt of local humour and created a safe refuge for the gangs of delinquents he hated so much. It was even possible to imagine him reaching an extremity in which he was prepared to destroy the building altogether . . .

The police car abruptly slowed down as the street ahead of it became congested with other vehicles and groups of pedestrians all, as though taking part in an animal migration, converging on the site of the hotel. Werry swore and rolled down his window as he came to an intersection where a uniformed police officer was absent-mindedly controlling traffic while exchanging banter with two girls.

"Arnold," he shouted, "stop trying to fix yourself up and get this street cleared right up to the hotel entrance. Do you hear me?"

Arnold gave him a friendly wave. "I hear you, Al. Some fun, eh?"

"That's what I have to work with," Werry muttered as he switched on the car's warning lights and forced his way at dangerous speed up to the hotel grounds and across the line of the perimeter fence. Several other cars and two fire vehicles were parked in a loose cluster a short distance away, their headlights streaking the grass. Werry slid his cruiser into place beside them and got out, smoothing his tunic as he craned his neck to look up at the hotel. Hasson joined him as he was met by the bear-like, sag-bellied figure of air patrolman Henry Corzyn.

"It doesn't look like there's much happening up there," Werry said.

"You can't see anything till you get up high." Corzyn lowered his voice and moved closer to Werry. "I haven't said anything to the television people, but I think there's a bunch of angels still in the building, Al. I got as close as I could and shone a light in, and I think I saw somebody skulking about. Couldn't be sure, though."

"Why don't they pull out? Aren't they worried about being roasted?"

"Who knows what goes on inside their pointed little heads?" Corzyn shifted his position until he had his back to a man who was standing nearby aiming a television camera at the sky. "Besides, if there's anybody dead up there . . ."

Werry looked at him with narrowed eyes. "Are you trying to make me feel good?"

"It was one hell of an explosion, Al. Most of the glass is gone out of the first floor windows on this side—and those kids don't go around singly, you know. A whole bunch of them might have got clobbered all at once."

Werry walked three paces away from Corzyn, stood for a moment with a hand on his brow, then came back. "That isn't very likely, is it? I mean, some of the others would have sent for help."

Corzyn shrugged. "Young Terry Franz from the TV station is up there now with a big spotlight. Maybe he'll be able to see more'n I could."

"You better get up there with him, Henry. Try to check the place out. Take a megaphone with you."

"Got one here." Corzyn touched his breast pocket, revealing the square outline of an electronic voice magnifier, and shifted his hand to the control panel of his CG harness. Hasson turned away, chilled, unable to watch the take-off. He waited a moment and when he directed his gaze skywards Corzyn's shoulder and ankle lights were like a small group of tracer bullets speeding towards the dim-glowing target of the hotel. The dinner Hasson had eaten became an unwanted mass in his stomach.

"Where's Quigg?" Werry bellowed, striding towards the nearest knot of onlookers. "Has anybody seen Victor Quigg?"

"Here I am, Al." Quigg, managing to appear thin and adolescent even when wearing a flying suit, detached himself from a group which was standing at a portable television transmitter. Werry gripped his arm and drew him into a private triad with Hasson.

"Victor," he said quietly, "are you making unauthorised statements to the gentlemen of the press?"

Quigg glanced at Hasson, obviously wondering how he fitted into the picture. "You know me better than that, Al."

"Okay. Did you tell anybody you saw Buck up at the hotel today?"

"Nobody 'cept Henry. He was the only one I told."

"Are you *sure* it was Buck you saw?"

Quigg nodded vigorously, jiggling the magnifying visor of his flying helmet. "It was Buck, all right. I had a second look at him because he was all rigged up with panniers and he don't usually like to load hisself down that way. He was taking something into the hotel."

Werry made a clicking noise with his tongue. "But you didn't try to find out what."

"It's his place, Al," Quigg said reasonably. "I figured he was entitled."

"You did right." Werry gave the young policeman a sombre stare. "I want you to keep quiet about this till I say it's all right to talk. Okay?"

"Sure, Al. By the way, nobody has contacted Lutze's folks yet—do you want me to do it?"

Werry frowned. "Lutze? Lutze?"

"Yeah—the kid who got hisself blown up. Didn't Henry tell you?"

"Is that Barry Lutze?"

"No such luck," Quigg said. "This is his cousin Sammy. The family lives out Bettsville direction. They probably didn't even know he was out of his own back yard tonight."

"Probably not," Werry agreed. "Call the station and get somebody down there to notify the Lutzes. I want you to stay here and . . ."

"Hey, *Al*!" One of the men at the television unit beckoned to Werry. "Come over and have a look at this, for God's sake—old Henry's trying to get into the hotel."

Werry mouthed an obscenity and ran towards the group who were gathered around a television monitor. Hasson, beginning to feel bemused, hurried in his wake. The console of the television unit was illuminated with greenish light, but recessed into it were three wells of blackness which housed solid-image monitors. In the centre one was a small vivid projection which showed Henry Corzyn moving against a background of the hotel's unevenly-lit outer surface. The image was drifting slightly, due to the fact that it was coming from a camera held by a flier, but it clearly showed a window whose lattice bars had been cut away to make an aperture large enough to admit a man.

Hasson watched in fascination, trying to ignore the queasiness in his stomach, as Corzyn swooped towards the window. The policeman went in fast, came within field interference distance of the wall and immediately began to drop. Hasson pressed his knuckles to his lips. Corzyn made a grab for the window frame, managed to get a handhold and checked his fall.

"That's his second shot at it," somebody commented admiringly. "Who'd have thought old Henry had it in him?"

The miniaturised Corzyn clung to the frame for a moment, breathing heavily, and dragged himself through the opening into the interior of the building. A second later his head and shoulders reappeared and he waved his hand at the camera, grinning like a sports idol. Hasson tilted his head back and tried to see the actual event, but he could discern only a tiny star-like glimmering in the remote high darkness.

Werry raised his wrist communicator to his lips. "Henry, what do you think you're doing? I sent you up there to look the place over—not to rupture yourself."

"It's all right, Al—I'm doing just fine." Corzyn sounded breathless but triumphant. "This window I'm at is on the second floor, so I'm above the fire. It doesn't seem like much of a fire, anyway—I might even be able to put it out."

"That's not your job."

"Relax, Al. I'm going to have a quick look around and make sure the place is empty. I'll have plenty of time to bail out if the fire gets worse. See you around!"

Werry lowered his wrist and stared accusingly at the man who had summoned him to the television unit. "This is your fault, Cec. Henry's way too old and tubby to be making grandstand plays. He'd never have done it if you hadn't been here."

"He'll be all right," Cec replied carelessly. "We'll give him an on-the-spot interview to himself when he comes down. Make his day for him."

"You're all heart." Werry moved away from the group, taking Hasson with him, and looked up into the night sky where aerial spectators had begun to congregate, swarming like fireflies.

"Here they come," he said. "The long-nosed rubbernecks—noted for their habit of gathering in large numbers at scenes of accidents, making loud honking noises and getting in everybody's way. It looks like the whole city will be here in a couple of minutes."

Hasson spoke in a low voice, choosing his words with the utmost care. "One citizen is notable by his absence."

"That's what I was thinking." Werry scratched the back of his head, a gesture which made him look boyish and handsome in the uncertain light. "Rob, there's no two ways about this, is there?"

Hasson shook his head, feeling a dreadful responsibility. "After the evidence you've heard, the very least you can do is talk to Morlacher."

"I guess it had to come to this some day." Werry glanced up at the hotel. "Things seem pretty quiet up there—I'll go and have a word with Buck now." He turned and walked away through the battery of golden headlight beams, casting multiple shadows on the broken ground.

Hasson stood and watched him depart, recounting to himself every one of his reasons for not getting involved, then he too walked towards the waiting police car.

CHAPTER 8

DURING THE DRIVE to the Morlacher house Al Werry produced the peaked and braided cap of his office—apparently it was a reserve he kept in the car for emergencies—and positioned it carefully on his head, leaning sideways to look at himself in the rear view mirror. It seemed to Hasson, watchful in the passenger seat, that he derived more reassurance from the resplendent headgear than from the pistol strapped to his side.

No other cars were visible when they emerged from the tunnel of shrubbery and crunched to a halt near the house's panelled front door, but rays of light slanting from the tall windows showed the place was occupied. Hasson got out of the police cruiser with Werry and stood for a moment looking around him. The view from the low crest was exactly as he had seen it before—the Chinook Hotel was not even visible beyond the heaped embers of the city—but to his imagination the atmosphere was entirely different. He had a disturbing sense of being watched.

"Do you think they know we're here?" he said.

"No doubt about it—Buck's a great man for surveillance systems." Werry went up the stone steps to the house, tugging, smoothing and adjusting his uniform in a manner which reminded Hasson of a peacock dressing its plumage. Hasson went with him, but hung back a little, suddenly aware that his own casual sweater and slacks could only detract from Werry's ritual show of authority. Werry touched a bell push and waited for the door to open. Hasson smiled encouragingly, but Werry regarded him with the cool blank eyes of a stranger and remained that way until they heard the sound of a lock being operated. The door opened a short distance to reveal the wisp-bearded face of Starr Pridgeon. He looked at Werry and Hasson for a moment without speaking, maliciously amused.

"I want to talk to Buck," Werry said.

"Buck doesn't want to talk to you. Bye, Al." Pridgeon closed the door, but Werry slid a gleaming boot forward and prevented it from nesting fully into the frame. The door opened again, and this time Pridgeon's face was slack-jawed with resentment.

"Al, why don't you do us all a big favour and stop trying to act like a real live cop?" he said with mock reasonableness. "You don't fool nobody—so why don't you just hop into your kiddycar and go back to where you came from?"

Werry moved forward a little. "I told you I want to talk to Buck."

Something flickered in Pridgeon's eyes. "I guess I can't stop you coming in—but just remember you weren't invited." He moved back and swung the door fully open, leaving the entrance clear.

Hasson, his instincts aroused, got the impression that Pridgeon had been uttering a rehearsed statement—like a junior barrister going over a point of law—and at the same time he noticed the odd waltz-like movement with which Pridgeon retreated, a right-angled three-step which kept his feet off the area just inside the threshold. He started forward, grasping for Werry's arm, but was a fraction of a second too late.

Werry stepped across the door sill, there was a sharp *splat* of released energy, and Werry sank to his knees. He remained kneeling for perhaps a second, shaking his head, then collapsed on to the parquet floor. His cap rolled a short distance on the polished wooden bricks.

"Deary me!" Pridgeon said, grinning. "Deary me! How unfortunate! Somebody must have left the intruder screen switched on." He moved back, doing nothing to assist the fallen man. A door opened further along the hall and three men came through it, one of them carrying a beer glass. They exchanged nudges and advanced to stand behind Pridgeon, looking expectant and slightly self-conscious.

"What happened to old Al?" one of them said. "Has he had one of his turns?"

"It must be his time of the month," Pridgeon replied, triggering yelps of laughter, before he fixed his bleak gaze on Hasson. "You! Al's cousin from England! Get him out of here—he's making the place untidy."

Hasson moved forward and paused on the threshold. "Are you inviting me in, and is the intruder screen switched off?"

"This one doesn't ever take any chances," Pridgeon said over his shoulder, and turned back to Hasson. "The screen's off now. It was a pure accident, Al barging into it like that. Just tell him that when he wakes up."

Hasson knelt beside Werry and looked down into his face. The policeman was conscious, but his eyes were dulled and bubbles of saliva winked at the corners of his mouth. Hasson knew he had been subjected to a paralysing neuro-shock which had rendered him helpless by temporarily widening most of the synaptic gaps in his body, and that it would be a minute or two before he would be able to walk unaided. He slid his hands under Werry's arms, dragged him to a high-backed chair at the side of the hall and wrested him onto it.

"Outside," Pridgeon commanded. "I told you to get him out of here."

"He isn't fit to go anywhere just yet." Kneeling beside the chair, Hasson patted Werry's cheeks with his left hand, while with his right he covertly unbuttoned the safety strap which held Werry's pistol in its holster. "The least you can do is give him a glass of water."

Pridgeon's lips tightened. "I'm giving you both ten seconds to get out of here."

"What'll you do then—send for the police?" Hasson renewed his efforts to give Werry control of his own body and was rewarded by a preliminary stirring of his limbs. Werry rolled his head from side to side, then brought his eyes to focus on Hasson's face.

"I'm sorry, Rob," he said thickly. "I . . . You'd better get me out to the car."

Hasson leaned forward and brought his mouth close to Werry's ear. "Al," he whispered urgently, "I know how sick you must feel. I know how little you want to hear all this right now, but if you leave this house without talking to Morlacher you're finished as a police officer. Too many people have seen what happened. They'll talk it up all over town, and you'll be *finished*."

Werry almost smiled. "Supposing I don't even care."

"You *do* care! Listen, Al, you don't even have to do anything. You don't even have to stand up—just talk to Morlacher the way you set out to do. Then we can leave. Okay?"

"Okay, but who's going to . . .?"

"That's it! I've had enough of you two pricks." Pridgeon's feet sounded on the floor behind Hasson. "Nobody can say I didn't give you a fair warning."

Hasson stood up and turned to face him. "Reeve Werry has deputised me to act for him—and we want to talk to Mr. Morlacher."

"He's deputised *you*!" Pridgeon gaped at Hasson, then he smiled and closed his eyes for a moment like a man experiencing a long-sought ecstasy. "Here's what I think of you, cripple."

Slowly and gently, as though about to pick up a priceless vase, he raised his hands towards Hasson's ears. Hasson placed one hand on the centre of Pridgeon's chest and gave him a stiff-armed shove which took him completely unawares, carrying him backwards too fast for his feet to catch up. He fell, sliding on his back on the polished floor with his legs in the air. One of the watching men gave a derisive whoop.

Pridgeon scrambled to his feet, mouthing venomously, and went for Hasson, this time coming in with all his speed, slit-eyed and crouching, determined to wreak swift and bloody vengeance for the humiliation he had just received. He feinted with his left and right, then threw a looping right-handed punch which was aimed at Hasson's throat.

Hasson, shifting into adrenalin overdrive, had time to analyse the three movements and knew at once that here was an instinctive and over-confident opponent, the sort of man who blundered casually into physical duels perhaps once a year—winning by dint of strength and ferocity—and who on that basis had deluded himself into believing he was a superior and gifted fighter. Lifting the punch harmlessly over his shoulder with his left forearm, Hasson saw the whole of Pridgeon's body hung up before him like an anatomical wall-chart with all the nerve centres marked in red, and made the discovery that he had no desire to bring the contest to a clean and scientific conclusion. Pridgeon had insulted him and degraded him and made him feel ashamed. Pridgeon liked tormenting blind youngsters who were in no position to do anything about it. Pridgeon liked using muscle on men he thought were cripples. For all that, and for a thousand other things of which Pridgeon had no knowledge, Pridgeon would have to pay a heavy price, and the time had come . . .

Hasson changed his point of aim and drove his right fist into Pridgeon's mouth, exulting in the dull snap of teeth. He threw Pridgeon against the panelled wall, to deny him the respite he might get through being knocked down, and hit him three more times, each time aiming for the face, each time connecting solidly and drawing blood. The madness boiled away as quickly as it had come when from the corner of his eye he detected a movement among the three men on his left. He allowed Pridgeon to slide down on to the floor and turned to face the men. They were advancing and fanning out to surround him, and on their faces was an expression Hasson had seen many times before—the righteous anger that a bully always feels when the victim has the temerity to strike back. The man with the beer glass—a stocky redneck in a plaid shirt—had drained the glass and was holding it with the base nestled into the palm of his hand.

Hasson moved in close to Werry and raised his hands like a traffic cop, giving them a signal to halt. "Before you men get yourselves involved," he said, forcing his voice to sound light and unconcerned, "I think you ought to know that Reeve Werry is here to make enquiries about a murder. Somebody planted a high-explosive bomb in the Chinook Hotel, and it went off a little while ago in the middle of a crowd of youngsters. More than one of them might be dead—we're not sure yet, but I can tell you that some people around here are going to go to jail for a long, long time. Now, it's up to you whether you want to dirty your hands with that sort of thing or not."

Hasson paused, breathing quietly and regularly to ease the pounding in his chest. The three men glanced at each other, obviously distrustful of Hasson and undecided about what to do next. His warning had been less effective than he had hoped it would be, and he had an uneasy feeling he was facing a group of individuals who had the classical criminal inability to weigh up future consequences.

"It's time somebody did somethin' about those punks up in the hotel," the man with the glass said. "They're nothin' but a pain in the ass."

"Yes, but is that any reason for you to become an accessory after the fact of murder?"

The man looked unconvinced. "That sounds like a load of bull to me. I don't know nothin' about no murder, but I know I don't like to see cops beatin' up on my friends."

"That's right," another man agreed, moving forward slightly.

"Look at it this way," Hasson said. "You came up here tonight to have a quiet drink and maybe a game of cards. Right? You didn't come out to get yourselves mixed up in a murder enquiry. It's a nasty business, and it could get even worse if this sort of thing was brought into it."

Hasson leaned sideways and drew Werry's pistol from its holster, holding the weapon between finger and thumb as if it was an object for which he had a deep distaste. He let the three look at it for several seconds, then lowered it back into the holster.

"I don't want to start waving a gun in your faces and perhaps have it go off by accident," he said. "I would hate that, and probably you would hate it even more, so why don't you go home and let Reeve Werry get on with what he came here to do?"

"What the man's saying is—take off while you're still able," Werry put in, rising to his feet. "It's good advice."

"We'll go if *you* say so, Al," one of the men growled. They lifted CG harnesses and suits which had been heaped untidily on a carved oak chest and filed out into the night. The last one out slammed the heavy door.

Hasson nodded to Werry, who was tentatively moving his shoulders. "Thanks, Al. I don't think I was getting through."

"Don't start thanking me, Rob—I'm not stupid." Werry brushed his uniform with his hands, picked up his cap and put it on. "I may be gutless, but I'm not stupid. Okay?"

"I don't think you know what gutless means. Remind me to tell you some time."

"Let's drop the subject," Werry said curtly, glancing at his communicator. "I wish I'd told Henry to keep in touch. I'd like to know if you're right about this being a murder gig."

"That was a dirty lie," Pridgeon came in unexpectedly, raising himself on to one elbow. His voice was indistinct, slurred through swollen lips, and his face had the blackened, dehumanised appearance Hasson had often noted on the features of accident victims. He was gazing at Hasson through bruised eyes which registered a mixture of hate, bafflement and accusation. Hasson stared him down, concealing a growing sense of guilt over having yielded to a dark and prehistoric instinct. Werry picked Pridgeon up by the lapels and swung him on to the chair he had just vacated.

"He told a dirty lie," Pridgeon mumbled. "You guys have some nerve coming in here and trying to make out that . . ."

"He told the truth," Werry cut in. "Somebody put a booby trap in the Chinook, and there's one kid hurt bad and maybe others dead, and there's only one man who would have had any reason to do a thing like that. Where's Buck? Is he in the house?"

"Buck's upstairs." Pridgeon gripped Werry's wrist and a plaintive note came into his voice. "Al, you wouldn't kid me, would you?"

"I'm not kidding you," Werry said impassively. "This is serious."

"Are you sure it wasn't just some little old blank shells or bird frighteners or something like that?"

"It was a high explosive. Do you know something about this, Starr? Because if you do . . ."

"I made up the fuses," Pridgeon said, wiping blood from his chin. "But Buck told me it was only . . ."

"Buck told you to keep your mouth shut." Morlacher, looking anachronistic in a traditional-style silk dressing gown, stepped off the bottom of a staircase at the end of the hall and walked towards the group. "Haven't you enough brains to know when you're being conned?"

Werry turned to him. "There's nobody being conned, Buck. Did you plant the bomb?"

"Of course not." Morlacher stooped to peer into Pridgeon's face, then gave Werry an incredulous smile. "Did you do that? You've just put yourself out of a job."

"It wasn't Al." Pridgeon pointed at Hasson. "He took a swing at me when I wasn't ready."

Hasson nodded. "Four times he wasn't ready."

"What's going on around here?" Morlacher said, frowning, switching his gaze between Werry and Hasson. "What do you two characters think you're playing at?"

"I asked you a question, Buck." Werry's voice was firm. "Did you plant that bomb?"

"I told you—I don't know anything about any bomb."

"You don't?" A light appeared in Werry's eyes. "Well, I'll tell you something about it. It has just set your frigging hotel on fire."

Morlacher's mouth contorted. "You're a liar."

"If you've got a pair of binoculars," Werry replied casually, "you can look out the window and see the inn on a pin turning into the fire on a spire."

"I've got to go there," Morlacher said, a pink triangle standing out on each cheek against the sudden pallor of his face. He turned and strode to the wooden chest which served as a hall table and picked up a CG harness.

Werry crossed to the entrance door and stood with his back to it, looking hard and confident behind the immaculate uniform and the badges of office, transformed into the man Hasson had once imagined him to be.

"I'll decide where you're going," he said. "After you've answered my questions."

"You, Al?" Morlacher continued struggling into the harness. "You're just a joke, and I'm in no mood for laughing right now." He tightened the harness's belt connection, took one pace towards the door and halted when he saw that Werry had drawn his pistol.

"What about the bomb?" Werry said.

"Now you're turning into a *bad* joke. You're not fooling anybody with that thing." Morlacher started to walk again.

Werry squeezed the trigger. There was no sound—the pistol was of a type which used electro-magnetic energy to expel its slugs—but a block leapt out of the parquet floor close to Morlacher's foot and skittered to the far end of the hall.

"The next one will go right up your nose," Werry promised. "Now—about this bomb . . ."

Morlacher took a deep breath, swelling hugely, as though sucking in elemental power for some Herculean feat of strength, then something seemed to break inside him. A driving force was neutralised, a puissance was withdrawn. He withered and shrank.

"For God's sake, Al," he pleaded, "what are you trying to do to me? Let me out of here. I've got to go to the hotel."

"About this bomb . . ."

"It wasn't meant to be a bomb." Morlacher spoke quickly, making fluttering movements with his hands. "You don't think I wanted to damage the hotel, do you?"

"What was it meant to be?"

"I just wanted to shake those punks up a bit. Scare them out of the place. Let me go now, Al."

Werry signalled his refusal with a movement of the pistol. "What did you use as an explosive?"

"It was just an old piece of hidyne I got from George York out at the Bettsville quarry."

"Hidyne! You used hidyne to scare kids?"

"Yes, but I cut it up into little squares."

"How little?"

"Little ones. *Little* ones! What more do you want me to say?"

"What weight were they?" Pridgeon shouted, lurching forward from his chair. "You didn't mention no hidyne to me. What weight were they?"

"How would I know?" Morlacher said impatiently. "Fifteen grammes. Twenty grammes. Something like that."

"Oh, Christ," Pridgeon quavered, turning towards Werry. "Al, I swear to you I didn't know about this. If there's anybody in the Chinook you better get them out of there. He got me to make up about twenty fuses."

"What sort of fuses are you talking about?" Werry said. "Do you mean timers?"

"Proximity fuses, Al. They'll fire off when anybody goes near them."

To Hasson's surprise, Werry seemed bemused by the incidental technicalities of what he had just heard. "But how could anybody work with a gadget like that? What's to stop it going off in your hand?"

"I used timers as well. The circuits are only activated at night." Pridgeon advanced on Werry, pressing both hands to his battered face as though holding it together. "Al, I had no *idea.*"

"Stay back," Werry told him, his eyes intent on Morlacher. "Buck, how many of those things did you actually put into the hotel?"

"All of them," Morlacher said in a dull voice.

"Whereabouts?"

"All over the place. One on each floor and a couple extra in places where I found food. You know, places where they've been camping out."

"Can you remember the exact locations?"

Morlacher shook his head. "The floors are mostly just wide open spaces. I'd need to look around in daylight."

"You've really done it, haven't you?" Werry fingered the controls of his communicator and raised it to his lips. "Victor? I was trying to raise Henry."

"I've been trying to contact him, too." Victor Quigg's voice sounded both tinny and anxious. "The first floor of the hotel is really alight now, Al. You can see the glow from down here on the ground—and if Henry doesn't get back to that second floor window soon he'll be in real trouble. The fire is going to cut him off, it looks like."

"Have you heard any more explosions?"

"Explosions? No, Al. What would . . .?"

"Victor, you've got to contact Henry," Werry said quickly. "Go up there with a voice magnifier, but don't go inside—the place is a minefield." He went on to explain the situation to Quigg, concluding with instructions to tell Henry Corzyn to retrace his exact path to the window by which he had entered.

"I'm on my way," Quigg said. "When are you coming back here, Al?"

"Soon." Werry's eyes, cold and unforgiving, remained fixed on Morlacher. "I've just one little chore to take care of first."

"Let's get out of here," Morlacher said in something like his normal manner, moving towards the door. "I've got to get to the hotel."

Werry continued to bar his way, shaking his head. "You're going to *my* hotel, Buck. I've got adjoining rooms reserved for you and Starr."

Morlacher pointed at him with an unsteady forefinger. "You've just lost yourself a good job."

"That's the second time in one night," Werry said, unimpressed. He took a pack of restraint patches from his pocket and tossed them to Hasson. "Behind their backs, Rob, if you don't mind. I don't want to take any chances."

Hasson nodded, went to Morlacher and drew the big man's hands together behind his back. He peeled the wrapper from a square blue patch, placed it between Morlacher's wrists and squeezed them together, creating an unbreakable bond. Pridgeon submitted to the same treatment almost eagerly, establishing himself as a man who believed in co-operating with the law.

"Now we can go," Werry said. He opened the front door, reconnecting the interior of the house to the outside universe, and this time the Chinook Hotel was immediately visible, burning low in the southern sky like a troubled red planet.

CHAPTER 9

AS WERRY HAD predicted, the vicinity of the hotel had become thronged with spectators, both on the ground and in the air. The roads bordering the hotel land swarmed with the glistening curvatures of automobiles, as though infested by monstrous insects, and the sky was filled with veering constellations of fliers' lights. A bilaser projector had been used to float a huge warning sign in the middle air, the crimson lettering of which read: CAUTION! THERE IS A DANGER OF MORE EXPLOSIONS! GLASS WILL FALL OVER A WIDE AREA! STAY CLEAR! And perched high on its unseen pinnacle, at the unmoving centre of the spangled chaos, the hotel building itself remained invisible except for a partial nimbus of flickering orange.

"I'm almost sorry I put Buck inside," Werry said as he got out of the police car. "He should have been here to see this."

Hasson tilted his head back, trying to take in the entire spectacle. "How long do you think he'll stay inside?"

"His lawyers should spring him in about an hour."

"It was hardly worth the trouble of putting him away."

"It was worth it to me—I owed him." Werry grinned vindictively. "Come on. I want to find out how Henry got on up there." He led the way across the uneven ground to where the impotent fire tenders stood in a line of other vehicles. The television unit was still in operation, surrounded by a cluster of men and women who were using its monitors to obtain a convenient view of the happenings in another world four hundred metres above their heads. As Werry and Hasson drew near, the slim figure of Victor Quigg detached itself from the group and came to meet them. His eyes had grown large and dark with strain, giving his immature face something of the look of a nocturnal animal.

"Everything okay?" Werry said. "Where's Henry?"

"Still up there, Al. I couldn't find him, and that's a fact."

"Do you mean he's still inside the hotel?"

"I guess so. He wouldn't have come out again without somebody noticing. He should have kept in touch." Quigg sounded tired and afraid.

"The crazy old . . ." Werry stood on his toes to get a glimpse of the television image of the hotel. "It looks like the fire will be through into the second floor in no time at all. How's he going to get back out?"

"That's what I want to know. Al, if anything happens to him . . ."

Werry silenced the young policeman by raising his hand. "Is there another way out of the hotel? What about the roof?"

"There must be a way in and out through the roof—that's the way the kids seem to get in—but I couldn't find it," Quigg said. "It's like a town up there, Al. All kinds of machinery houses and water tanks and things."

"Well, we can send for keys or rip a door off." Werry paused, looking thoughtful. "Except . . . if we go inside and start working down we're likely to stand on one of Buck's Goddam bombs. We might just have to take that risk."

"Henry should have kept in touch."

"What about the windows?" Hasson put in. "Are there no big ones he can put out with a brick?"

Werry shook his head morosely. "It's all this modern blast-proof —blast-proof, that's a good one—tessellated stuff. They're supposed to make high buildings more psychologically acceptable, or something like that."

"I see." Hasson moved closer to the television unit and examined the image being sent down by the airborne camera operator. The architect of the Chinook Hotel had extended the tessella motif to the entire outer surface, blending walls and windows into a single mosaic design. Looked at from a purely aesthetic point of view the building was a success, and it would have been unfair to expect an architect to foresee a situation in which anybody would have wanted to launch himself out of a room into the sort of thin cruel air streams that flowed over and above the Empire State Building. Hasson's imagination, catching him off guard, drew him into the situation he had envisaged and the ground seemed to rock beneath his feet. He turned away from the television monitor, sickened, and was trying to control his breathing when he saw a young woman approaching from the direction of the road. Seeing her in the unusual circumstance and setting, he had a momentary difficulty in identifying her as May Carpenter. She hurried by him, white-faced and distraught, and halted beside Al Werry.

Werry put an arm around her shoulders and turned her towards the road. "You can't stay here, honey. It's dangerous and right now I'm . . ."

"Theo's gone," she said in a taut unhappy voice. "I can't find him anywhere."

"He'll have slipped out with some of his pals," Werry soothed. "I'll talk to him about it later."

May shook free of his arm. "I've called around everywhere. All the places he goes. Nobody has even *seen* him tonight."

"May," Werry said impatiently, "can't you see I'm kind of busy?"

"He's up there." Her words were measured, unaccented, made lifeless by the weight of certainty. "He's up there in the hotel."

"That's a stupid thing to say. I mean, it's just . . . *stupid*."

May pressed the back of a hand to her forehead. "He goes out flying some nights with Barry Lutze, and that's where they always go—up into the hotel."

"You don't know what you're talking about," Werry said.

"It's true."

"If you knew that, and didn't tell me," Werry replied, his face suddenly inhuman, "you've killed him."

May closed her eyes and sagged to the ground. Hasson moved in and caught her at the same time as Werry, and between them they bore her a few paces and seated her on the footplate of a nearby truck. Several men looked round curiously and tried to move closer, but Quigg spread his arms and shepherded them away.

"I'm sorry, I'm sorry, I'm sorry," May whispered. "I'm so *sorry*."

Werry cupped her face in his hands. "I shouldn't have said a thing like that. It's just that . . . It's just that . . . May, why didn't you tell me? Why didn't you let me know?"

"I tried to, but I couldn't."

"I don't get it," Werry said, almost to himself. "I don't get this at all. If it had been anybody but Theo . . ."

Hasson felt something heave in his subconscious. "Did he go for the drugs, May? Was he taking empathin?"

She nodded and a thin glaze of tears appeared on her cheeks.

"Why did he do that, May?" Hasson said, ideas crystallising in his mind. "Could he see when he was taking empathin?"

"I couldn't understand it," she said, opening her eyes and gazing sadly at Werry. "I caught him going out through his bedroom window one night and I was going to tell you, but he begged me not to. He told me that when he's with the other kids and they're all taking empathin he sometimes gets to see what they can see. He said it comes in flashes. He talked about telepathy and things like that, Al, and he was so desperate and it meant so much to him, and I one time heard you saying that empathin and gestaltin and stuff like that doesn't do anybody any harm . . ."

"I said that, did I?" Werry said slowly, straightening up. The communicator on his wrist began to buzz, but he appeared not to notice. "I suppose anybody can make a mistake."

May looked up at him in supplication. "He hates living in the dark."

"You know what has happened here?" Werry said, adjusting the angle of his cap, slipping back into his old role. "We're jumping to a conclusion. We're making one hell of a big jump to a conclusion—there's no proof that there's *anybody* up in the hotel. Anybody apart from Henry Corzyn, that is."

Victor Quigg moved closer, fluttering his fingers to attract Werry's attention. "Al, would you like to answer your radio? I think something has happened."

"There we are," Werry said triumphantly. "This'll be Henry telling me he has checked the place out."

"I don't think it's Henry," Quigg mumbled, looking deathly pale.

Werry gave him a questioning glance and raised his communicator to his lips. "Reeve Werry speaking."

"You shouldn't have done it, Werry." The voice from the radio was laboured, the words coming in ponderous succession as though each one had to be examined and checked for meaning before being assembled into the overall message. "You did bad things this day."

Hasson lowered his wrist a little and looked at the radio in bafflement. "Is that Barry Lutze?"

"Never mind who it is. I'm just letting you know that everything that happened tonight was your fault. You're the killer, Werry—not me. Not me." Listening to the painfully enunciated words and phrases, Hasson guessed the speaker had been seriously injured. He also developed a dark conviction that a new element of dread was being added to an already nightmarish situation.

"Killer? What's this about killer?" Werry grasped the side of the truck. "Wait a minute! Was my boy up there? Was Theo hurt?"

"He was here when your bomb went off. You didn't expect that, did you, Mister Werry?"

"Is he all right?"

There was a prolonged, pulsing silence.

"Is he all right?" Werry shouted.

"He's with me now." The voice was grudging, heavy with resentment. "You're lucky—he's in good shape."

"Thank God for that," Werry breathed. "And how about Officer Corzyn?"

"He's with me, too—but he isn't in good shape."

"What do you mean?" Werry demanded, his eyes brooding and speculative.

"I mean he's dead, Mister Werry."

"Dead?" Werry glanced up at the hotel, now visible as a black disk surrounded by a thin corona, like a moon eclipsing a reddish sun. "What are you doing with Corzyn's radio, Lutze? Did you kill him?"

"No, *you* killed him." The voice had begun to sound agitated. "It was your fault for sending a fat, soft old guy like that in here after me. I only hit him once and . . ." There was a moment of silence, and when the voice resumed speaking the flat inhuman quality had returned to it. "You should have come up here and done your own dirty work, Mister Werry. I wouldn't have minded taking you on. Not one bit."

"Take it easy, Lutze—let's try to get some sense into this conversation before it's too late," Werry said. "What am I supposed to have done tonight? What have you got against me?"

"The bomb, Mister Reeve Werry. The bomb!"

Werry stamped the ground. "Is that some kind of sick joke? Are you still swallowing cuckoo capsules up there, Lutze? Buck

Morlacher planted that bomb, and you damn well know it."

"What's the difference? You work for him, don't you?"

"I don't work for him," Werry said, bringing his voice under control. "I just got back here from throwing him into a cell."

"Big deal," the voice sneered. "He'll do an hour—with twenty minutes off for good behaviour. The way I see it, that doesn't seem enough for murdering my cousin and smashing up my ribs."

"Young Sammy isn't dead. He's in hospital, but he isn't dead."

There was a lengthy silence, a pause in the verbal duel, then the unseen speaker made the next logical move. "The fat cop is dead."

Werry took a deep breath. "Listen to me, Barry. If you didn't intend to cause Henry Corzyn's death, that changes things. We can talk about it later. Right now the only thing on my mind is making sure that nobody else gets hurt or killed. Are you listening to me?"

"I'm listening."

"What you've got to know is that Buck planted about twenty of those booby traps all over the hotel. They're on every floor, and they've got special fuses to trigger them off if you even get close. Where are you now?"

"Third floor."

"Well, you've got to bring Theo down to the second-floor window, the one with the hole in it. Only walk in places you've already been today. Come out through the window, and we'll take it from there."

"Take it from there!" The radio on Werry's wrist emitted a humourless laugh which ended in a wheeze. "I'll bet you would. You'd like that, wouldn't you?"

"You've got no choice," Werry said. "It's the only thing you can do."

"No deal, Mister Werry. I'm not even sure I could reach that window—things are getting pretty hot down there. And even if I could, I don't think I could jump out far enough to clear my field. I'm bound to drop way down below the first floor before I can pick up any lift."

"Nobody will interfere with you in any way. All I want is to get Theo out of there. I swear to you. I swear to you, Barry, I'll give you any guarantee you want."

"Save your breath, Mister Werry—we're going up to the roof. I can be sure of getting away from up there, and I'll be in Mexico by tomorrow."

"You can't do that," Werry said, beginning to pace in frantic circles in a manner which pained Hasson to watch. "Use your brains, man."

"That's what I'm doing," the voice assured him. "For all I know, those other bombs don't exist—but, even if they do, this is a pretty big place and I've got myself a pathfinder. Theo can go in front."

Werry stopped pacing. "I warn you—don't do this."

"Now, I don't want you to worry about a thing, Mister Werry." The voice was elated, nervous, mocking. "Theo and I are going for a quiet little stroll up to the roof. With any luck, you can pick him up there in about five minutes. Just make sure nobody tries to pick *me* up, that's all—I've got the fat guy's gun and I know how to use it."

"Lutze! *Lutze*!" Werry squeezed the instrument on his wrist as though trying to force it to respond, but the radio link had been broken. May Carpenter covered her face and gave a low sob. Werry traced the outline of a CG harness on his torso with a finger and pushed Quigg away in the direction of his car. Quigg nodded understandingly and ran. Werry strode to the television unit and the group around it melted out of his way.

"What are things like on the second floor?" he said. "Can I still get in that window?"

"See for yourself, Al." The technician in charge pointed at the image of the lower section of the hotel. All the visible windows of the first floor were blocked in with sheets of flame which were turning from orange to a searing white. "You could probably get in, but that second floor looks like it's about to cave in at any second."

"I better go in higher up." Werry ran to a fire truck and returned some seconds later carrying the bayonet-like shape of a thermal cutter. Victor Quigg met him with his CG harness and handed it over without speaking. Hasson stood by, his mind lurching out over dizzy chasms each time he thought of Werry's intention, and watched him pull the broad straps tight around his body. He felt weak-kneed and helpless, and—in some indefinable way—responsible for the other man's plight.

Werry gave him a grim smile as he made the last connection. "Here it is again, Rob—no two ways."

"I don't know," Hasson said, donning the mantle of Judas. "It may not do any good to bull your way in. There are so many things that could . . . I mean, it might be better to wait."

"The way you would do if it was your son up there?"

Hasson backed away, ashamed and afraid, as Werry switched on his lights, moved a control on the harness's waist panel and made an easy leap into the air. He went up fast, falling into the sky, a dwindling light, a star being recalled to the rightful business of stars. Far above, as though making ready to receive him in battle, the black disk of the hotel building hurled out a streamer of yellow fire from its south side. The outburst, a solar prominence in miniature, faded almost at once and the watchers on the ground heard a dull powdery report. Quigg snatched his voice magnifier from his pocket.

"That was another bomb," he announced, already an expert. "Watch out for glass!"

Hasson ran with the others and pressed into the lee of a fire appliance, and a surprisingly long time later there was a brief, irregular pattering and whispering in the grass all around. As soon as it felt safe he returned to the television unit. The pyrotechnics which had accompanied the blast indicated that it had occurred on the blazing first floor—but he wanted to be sure that Al Werry had ascended safely through the wind-scattered hail of glass fragments.

Cec, the chief technician, switched on a microphone circuit. "Terry, look out for Al Werry arriving up there. He's got a cutter with him, and he's about to try going in one of the upper windows. We're gonna get some good network footage out of this, so stick with him. Right?"

"Right, Cec," came Terry Franz's reply and the image in the monitor well swung giddily. It centred on the figure of Werry who was silhouetted for an instant against the inferno on the hotel's first floor before reaching the darker background of the levels above. Hasson felt an absurd constriction in his throat as he noticed that Werry, contravening police flight regulations, was wearing his ornate cap in place of a helmet.

Werry brought himself into the hovering mode about five

metres out from a fourth-floor window and drew his pistol. He aimed it and fired, and the camera—with its superb low-light vision—showed a hole appearing in one of the square panes. Werry kept on firing, always hitting the same small rectangle, until it had been cleared of glass. He put the gun back in its holster and worked at the controls of the thermal cutter, bringing a dagger of diamond-sharp brilliance into being at its tip. Without hesitation, Werry moved further out from the wall of the hotel, gaining a little extra height as he went. The headlights of the cars on the ground far below slid into view under his feet, tiny out-of-focus candle flames.

Werry altered a belt control and swooped in towards the window. As soon as he got within field interference radius he began to fall, but he had accurately compensated for the drop and he was able to thrust his left arm through the aperture he had created. His feet scrabbled for purchase on the horizontal divisions between tiles. He obtained a foothold, steadied himself and brought the cutter in his right hand into contact with the window frame. Its sun-white tip slid easily through metal and glass, tracing an orange-glowing line. Werry, clinging tightly to the sheer surface, began to extend the incision. The winds of altitude tugged at his uniform, producing a cold, welling nausea in Hasson's stomach.

Hasson turned away, wondering if he was actually going to vomit, but checked himself as he noticed a flurry of movement in the dimness beyond Werry's spreadeagled figure. A man in an unmarked flying suit was briefly seen, face a pale triangular blur, right arm extended. Hasson gave an involuntary shout as Al Werry tumbled backwards away from the window, the thermal cutter flying from his grasp and plunging out of sight. Werry fell a short distance, but his lateral impetus carried him out of interference range and his body began to float away on the night wind, limbs making feeble and uncoordinated movements. His cap fluttered down into the waiting darkness, like an escaping bird.

The menacing rectangular cavern of the window was empty once more.

For Hasson, there followed an agonised period of confusion in which he was only dimly aware of Victor Quigg leaping skywards, already paying out a plasteel line from the dispenser at his waist. Men shouted near him, but their voices were strangely distant. Myriad specks of brilliance wheeled in the overhanging night. Quigg reappeared, looking like an old man, towing an inert shape which many hands reached for as it neared the ground and became heavy, sagging down on to the grass.

Suddenly Hasson was kneeling beside Werry, staring in heart-thundering dismay at the bullet hole in the policeman's left shoulder. The location of the wound—just above the armpit—made it look relatively harmless, the sort of injury which would have drawn scarcely a wince from a character in a holoplay, but the entire left side of Werry's tunic was sodden with blood, glistening like a mass of fresh liver. Werry's face was almost luminescent in its pallor. His drifting gaze triangulated on Hasson and his lips began to move. Hasson bent lower in response to the inaudible plea.

"It all piles up on you," Werry whispered. "It's funny how it all . . ."

"Don't talk," Hasson urged. "Don't try to say anything."

Werry took his hand in a fragile grip. "You're not going to believe this, Rob, but I'm not even . . . I'm not even worried about . . ." A silence and a stillness descended over him, and his fingers relaxed their grip on Hasson's hand.

Hasson stood up and looked about him with burning, tear-prismed eyes. A man waiting nearby handed him Werry's cap, which had somehow terminated its descent in the immediate area. Victor Quigg rose from his kneeling position, snatched the cap and placed it on Werry's chest. He stood over the body for a few seconds, then turned and walked away in the direction of the nearest police car, trailing leaden feet through the long grass. Hasson ran after him and caught his arm.

"Where are you going, Victor?" he said.

"I want my shotgun," Quigg replied woodenly. "I'm going up on the roof of the hotel, and I'm going to wait there with my shotgun."

"Lutze mightn't even reach the roof."

"If he does, I'll be there with my shotgun."

"It's young Theo I'm thinking about now," Hasson said, hearing his own words across bleak interstellar distances. "Give me a gun and a spare harness."

CHAPTER 10

NOTHING IS HAPPENING. *I'm still on the ground—safe and secure. Nothing is happening.*

Hasson watched the underside of the Chinook Hotel blossom and unfurl like a carnivorous flower. As the circular building expanded to the limits of his field of view he began to see details of its structure—the spray of radial cantilevers, the spider-web pattern of ribs and intercostals, the twin circular apertures of the elevator shafts, one of which glowed with a shifting ruddy light which made it a back door to hell.

It's quite simple, you see. The foundation for the supporting column was positioned over a geological fault, or a swamp, and now the whole thing is sinking into it like a piston. I'm still on the ground—safe and secure—watching the hotel drop down to my level.

His flight brought him close to the hotel's lower rim and for the first time he was able to hear the fire at work. It was making little downward progress for the time being—only a few gleaming razor slashes revealed that beams and slabs were being tortured by heat and heat-induced stresses—but flames and hot gases were pouring up through stairwells and ventilation shafts to reach other floors, and their advance was signalled by ragged explosions of timbers, glass and paint containers. Clouds of smoke interspersed with streamers of long-lived sparks were being carried away on the wind.

It's quite fascinating—almost a privilege, really, though rather a ghoulish one—to be able to stand here on the ground and get such a good view of what is happening to the hotel. One can't help being reminded of the destruction of the Hindenburg. All the same, even though I'm safe and secure on the ground, that second floor window is getting very close, and if I'm to pop inside, casually, just for a quick look around I'd better think about how I'm going to . . .

Hasson hit the window frame hard, his ballistic-style ascent carrying him through the field interference phase with virtually no loss of speed. He gripped the alloy which trimmed the aperture where six panes had been cut out, his feet found slithering purchase on the edge of nothingness, and suddenly he was inside the hotel, breathing deeply, standing on a litter-strewn composition floor. The noise of the fire was much louder here and he could feel its heat striking up through the soles of his shoes. It occurred to him that the floor structure in that area could not survive for many more minutes.

He scanned his surroundings—peripherally aware of the television camera-man hovering in the airy asylum beyond the windows—and made out the sawtooth silhouette of a nearby staircase. Only major load-bearing walls had been completed throughout the hotel, and Hasson received a powerful impression of vastness, of being on a battlefield at night, where dozens of minor skirmishes were marked by transient glows and glimmers among forests of columns. He ran to the staircase and sprinted up it.

The thermal cutter he had tucked into his belt felt secure at his left side, but the pistol began to loosen due to the action of his body and he took it into his right hand. It was almost certain that Lutze and Theo Werry had preceded him on the same route, and therefore he felt safe from booby traps and their proximity fuses, but the time had come to prepare for an encounter with Lutze himself. He had been on the fourth floor when he shot Al Werry, but his climb to the roof of the hotel would have been hampered by his own injuries and, presumably, by the fact that Theo would be moving slowly in the lead. Hasson estimated that he could catch up on the pair as early as the eighth floor. He made sure the pistol's safety catch was off and began to count the floors as he pounded his way upwards through the Vulcanian dimness.

Four flights of steps to each floor, which means I'm on . . . Or is it only three flights? Perhaps I'm further up than I . . .

Hasson and Barry Lutze saw each other in the same instant.

Lutze was standing on a broad expanse of landing, looking upwards to where the stooped figure of Theo Werry was feeling his way to the top of a flight of bare steps which were made hideously dangerous by the absence of an outer banister. As soon as Lutze became aware of Hasson he dropped on one knee and began firing with the police weapon he had taken from Henry Corzyn. Hasson, still sliding to a halt, had no place to hide, no time to cry out or plan tactics. There could be nothing but the basic survival reaction. He raised his own pistol and worked the trigger as rapidly as its mechanism would permit, filled with the sick realisation that he had blundered into what some would describe as a fair fight, a classic stand-off whose result would be determined as much by the blindly spinning cylinders of chance as by personal attributes of the contenders. The pistol recoiled against his hand again and again, but never quickly enough, with a seeming aeon between each silent propulsive shock.

Two things occurred at once. A bomb detonated on a lower floor, sending a sheet of amber and red flame billowing up through a central well; and in the same instant—as though he had been caught in the blast—Lutze was flicked on to his back. Stress waves raced through the building, rippling the floor slabs and initiating a train of lesser explosions, but Lutze did not move. Hasson ran up to the landing, gun self-consciously at the ready. Lutze was lying with both hands clapped to his forehead, eyes glazed and unseeing, mouth locked open in an expression of frozen surprise.

Hasson turned away from him and saw that Theo Werry had fallen to his knees. The boy was only centimetres from the naked rim of a man-made abyss which terminated many floors below, and he was unsteadily rising to his feet. Hasson opened his mouth to shout a warning, but a vision of what might happen if he startled Theo sprang into his mind. He bounded up the stairs, threw an arm around Theo and dragged him away from the edge. The boy began to fight against him.

"It's all right, Theo," Hasson said firmly. "This is Rob Hasson."

Theo ceased to struggle. "Mr. Haldane?"

"That's what I meant to say. Come on—we're getting out of here." Hasson gripped a strap of the boy's harness and began drawing him down to the landing he had just quit. He guided him past Lutze's body, and away from the yawning mouth of the stairwell, to a window in the outer wall. The dark world beyond looked peaceful, sane and inviting. Hasson shoved the pistol into a pocket, took the thermal cutter from his belt and set its controls.

"I don't get it," Theo said, his face turning from side to side. "How did you get here?"

"Same way as you did, son."

"But I thought you couldn't fly."

"I've done a bit in my time." Hasson activated the cutter, turning it into a sorcerer's sword of white fire.

Its light showed up the strain on Theo's dirt-streaked face. "What happened to Barry?"

"He had a gun. He started shooting at me, and I had to shoot back." Praying that Theo would not pursue the line of questioning, Hasson turned to the window and slid the tip of the cutter through the nearest pane. It went into the glass with scarcely any resistance, causing roseate glowing drops to course down the surface.

"I heard my father shouting something at me a few minutes ago," Theo said, raising his voice above the background noises in the building. "Where is he now?"

"We'll talk about that later, Theo—the main thing to worry about right now is . . ."

"Did Barry shoot him?"

"I . . . I'm afraid that's what happened." Hasson moved the blade of the cutter sideways and sliced through a bar of alloy. "Listen, Theo, I'm cutting us an escape door in a window and we're going to be out of here in a minute or two. I want you to get yourself ready to fly."

Theo felt for his arm and gripped it. "He's dead, isn't he?"

"I'm sorry—yes." Unable to look at the boy, Hasson concentrated all his attention on the window and felt a dull puzzlement when he saw that a small circular hole had appeared in one of the panes close to his face. The turmoil of his thoughts—about Al Werry and his son and the need to get away from the burning hotel—was so great that the sudden presence of the hole in the glass was an irrelevancy, or at most a fringe phenomenon of little importance. Was the heat from the cutter distorting the window frame and causing . . .?

A second hole appeared in the glass, and an incredible thought was born in Hasson's mind.

He spun round and saw Barry Lutze on his feet on the landing. Lutze still had one hand pressed to his forehead, his face was a fearsome bloody mask, and he was using the gun—the gun Hasson had neglected to kick clear of his body. In the act of turning Hasson, driven by pure instinct, hurled the thermal cutter. It flew in a series of eccentric whirls like a binary sun spinning around an invisible companion, touched Lutze's side, clattered down on to the floor in a fountain of sparks and disappeared into the open pit of the stairwell. Lutze, who had already been lurching unsteadily, fell to the floor. A single convulsive twitch flailed his four limbs simultaneously, then he was motionless, converted in an instant from a human being into something that could have no connection with life.

Hasson, who had been under the impression that the cutter had practically missed Lutze, ran to the body. The fleeting contact, the casual feather-flick from the sun-blade, had gouged a diagonal, smoking, ruinous furrow through Lutze's chest. This time, it was obvious, there was no need to deprive him of weaponry. Suppressing his natural reactions, Hasson strode to the stairwell and looked down, searching for the cutter, but was unable to see it. There was nothing but a complex tunnel of descending perspectives, obscured by smoke and patchily lit by shafts of hellish light. Swearing hopelessly, he ran back to Theo, who was still standing by the window looking stunned and frightened.

"We've lost the cutter," Hasson said, trying to keep the panic out of his voice. "Do you know the way out of here?"

Theo shook his head. "There's a door in the roof somewhere, but I couldn't find it. Somebody always led me in and out."

Hasson weighed the odds, balancing one vision of dread against another, and came to a decision. "Come on, son, we're going down and we've got to go *fast.*"

He took Theo's hand and dragged him towards the stairs. The boy tried to hang back, but Hasson was too strong for him and in a few seconds they were committed to a perilous plunge into the noisome lower regions of the hotel. Having surrendered himself, Theo did his best to match strides with Hasson, but the task was an impossible one for a blind person and their descent became a sequence of mutual collisions, near-falls and extended ankle-twisting slides. Only the fact that the banisters had been installed on those flights saved them from disastrous spills into the central well.

With each successive landing the heat, fumes and noise grew more intense, and when they finally reached the second floor Hasson was appalled to find that it had begun to disintegrate. Some of the slabs were humped like sand dunes and beginning to glow at the edges. Violent tremors coursed through the structure, accompanied by awesome low-frequency groans which suggested that the floor would fall through at any second.

Hasson pushed Theo towards the aperture in the large window. He gripped the boy by the shoulders and turned him round to face him, at the same time activating his CG unit. The function light on the control panel at Theo's waist remained dead. Hasson's gaze traced a practised line over Theo's flight equipment, and came to a foundering halt at the clips which should have held the power pack. He felt his face contort with shock.

"Theo!" he shouted, thunderstruck by the magnitude of the discovery. "Your power pack! Where's your power pack?"

Theo's hand groped around the empty clips. "Barry took it . . . Mexico . . . I forgot."

"It's all right—there's no harm done." Hasson found his lips dragging themselves into the wan semblance of a smile at the inappropriateness of his words as he disconnected his own power pack and fastened it to Theo's harness.

"I just forgot," Theo said. "When I heard about Dad . . . What are we going to do?"

"We're getting out of here, as planned," Hasson told him. "You're going first and I'll come after you when I grab another pack."

Theo's face turned towards the blazing interior of the hotel, blind but cognisant. "How can you . . .?"

"Don't argue," Hasson ordered, completing the electrical connections and bringing the vital pea-sized dome of radiance into being at Theo's waist.

"We could try it together," Theo said. "I've heard about people going piggyback."

"Kids." Hasson pushed him into the rectangular aperture. "Not grown men like us, Theo. Together we'd be way outside basic modular mass. And anybody's who's as keen on flying as you are ought to know all about BMM and field collapse."

"But . . ."

"Outside! I've set you at what ought to be just under height maintenance power for your weight, so when you get out there just let yourself float away and sink. Now . . . *go!*" Hasson shoved Theo as hard as he could, sending the boy tumbling into the cool black sanctuary of the night sky. Theo, feeling himself topple, added the impulsion of his own legs, turning his exit into a kind of sprawling dive which carried him well beyond field interference radius, out above the jewelled geometries of the city. He swam in a soft sea of air.

Hasson watched him curve away out of sight, then became aware that the floor slab under his feet had begun to shudder and stir like something possessed of life. He moved off it towards the stairs, feeling curious rather than immediately threatened, and in that instant the slab exploded into fragments. Some pieces fell to the floor below, others were carried upwards in a roaring gout of fire which made the landing as bright as day and seared the moisture from Hasson's eyes. He threw himself on to the staircase and ran for the upper floors, expecting at any second to find himself treading empty space. Other ominous rumbles coupled with an increase in the general brightness told him that the structure of the hotel was beginning to succumb to the onslaught on an increasing scale.

He tried to increase his speed, forcing his thighs to reach high with every stride, and his breath began to come in raucous, throat-tearing gasps. When he had been running for what felt like a very long time a new fear began to manifest itself, a fear that he might unwittingly have passed the level on which Lutze's body lay. Or, *or*, supposing that Lutze had managed to survive a second apparently mortal wound, even for a short time, and was no longer on the landing? Looking upwards, Hasson saw that he was reaching the point where the metal banister ceased to skirt the edge of the stair and he was able to establish his position. He stiff-armed himself away from the wall on to the next expanse of floor and experienced a moment of profound relief when he picked out the inert form of Lutze lying exactly where he had last seen it.

Crossing to the body, he dropped on to his knees and cast about him, expecting to locate the oblong mass of Theo's power pack either in Lutze's clothing or on the floor nearby. He was unable to find it. He raised his head and extended the scope of his search, only to discover that in the fitful and uncertain light every piece of litter and builder's rubble promised to be a power pack and almost immediately revealed itself to be something else.

A bomb exploded on one of the floors he had passed seconds earlier, producing the now-familiar upsurges of flame and horizontal billowings of dust and smoke. Accompanying the blizzard of paper and plastic scraps there came a heaving of the floor, an uneasy sense of loosening.

Hasson realised that even in the period of dire extremity he had been indulging one part of his nature, claiming the luxury of fastidiousness. He rolled Lutze's body on to its side, exposing the black-lipped obscenity of the fatal wound, and unclipped the power pack from the dead man's harness. The unit itself and the electrical connectors were slimed with dark blood. Hasson stood up, clutching the unit to his chest, and loped wearily towards the stairs.

His upward progress was now complicated by the absence of a banister. The prolonged and punishing exertion was robbing his legs of both strength and control. There was an increasing tendency for his knees to buckle and for his feet to come down some distance from their point of aim—but with no balustrade at his side the slightest stumble could have resulted in a one-way trip to the inferno of the first floor. Into the bargain, he was now in a section of the hotel which, for all he knew, had not been traversed since Morlacher had planted his over-powered booby traps, which meant there was a new risk of being swatted into oblivion by an unseen hand. The remnants of his powers of thought told him it was a hazard that would have to be accepted—to get out of the hotel he would have to go all the way to the roof and find the exit used by Barry Lutze and the other aerial trespassers. It was a dismal and dangerous prospect, but the only one open to him.

Having managed to project his thoughts a short distance into the future, Hasson—above the agonised pumping of his thighs and the bellows-sound of his breathing—began to speculate about whether the stair he was climbing would terminate in a doorway to the roof. There had been plans for roof gardens and swimming pools, so it was likely that there would be provision for public access by stair as well as by the elevator service. Spurred on by the hope of perhaps suddenly and easily finding himself outside in the clean starry air, Hasson turned his gaze upward, wondering if he would be able to identify the top landing when it came into view.

In the event there was no difficulty. The entire top storey of the hotel was filled with an impenetrable, rolling layer of smoke and fumes which extended almost from floor level up to the invisible ceiling.

Hasson sank down, winded, on the flight of steps which slanted on to the uppermost floor, feeling like a man under siege as he took stock of his surroundings. The underside of the metres-thick blanket of smoke was defined with surprising sharpness. It shifted and heaved and puckered like the surface of a slow-boiling soup which was being seen through an inverting lens, and there was a thin stratum of clear air between it and the floor. Peering horizontally through the translucent sandwich, Hasson was able to discern the beginnings of yet another flight of steps at the opposite side of the landing. The treads were narrower than those upon which he sat, and the conviction grew in him that they led directly to a door which opened on to the hotel roof.

He forced himself to remain at rest for the space of a few more breaths, gathering oxygen into his system, then he stood up, locked his chest muscles, and ran for the ascending stairway. His feet found the steps, seemingly without his guidance, and he hurled himself blindly upwards, going as fast as he could, aware that even one inhalation of the reeking blackness surrounding him could result in calamity. Almost at once a new thought occurred—how could he be sure that the stairs he was now on followed the same layout as those below? How did he know he was not about to plunge over an unguarded edge? Fending the thought off he kept running, trailing a hand along a rough-cast wall, until he reached a small landing and a metal door. The door was bolted, padlocked, immovable.

Almost grateful that the door, because of its patent solidity, had not tempted him to waste time in trying to force it, Hasson turned and ran back the way he had come. He reached his starting point just as his lungs were giving out and hunkered down on the steps. Tatters of acrid smoke clinging about him flayed his nostrils and throat, triggering a bout of coughing. He clung to the steps until the convulsions ended, a part of his mind disdaining involvement, using the moments of astral detachment to analyse the situation.

From the moment he had entered the Chinook Hotel his life had depended on interplays of forces. Some of the factors he had contended with had been human, others had been purely physical—and not all of them had worked entirely to his disadvantage. The design and topography of the building, for example, had conspired to give him some respite, some time to manoeuvre. A fire was like a primeval jet engine, needing air intakes and an efficient exhaust before it could attain its full deadly splendour. The fact that the roof of the hotel remained unvented and intact—as evidenced by the trapped pall of smoke—had denied the fire the upward exhaust it craved, slowing its progress, cramping its natural style. Had the layer of smoke and fumes not been able to form, he, Rob Hasson, would no longer be alive, having been engulfed and incinerated at a much earlier stage. It was unfortunate—though no indication of malice on the part of the physical world—that the same toxic cloud was now making it impossible for him to search for the only escape route to the outside universe . . .

Far below Hasson a cataclysm overtook part of the edifice of sloping stair beams upon which he was poised. There was a gargantuan shuddering and thundering which suggested that whole flights of stairs were breaking free of their supports and dropping like carelessly released playing cards. Currents of hot gas geysered up through the central well beside him, churning the overhanging canopy of smoke.

Hasson uttered an involuntary moan as the staircase on which he was perched gave a tentative lurch. He crawled forward on to the floor proper, pressing himself downwards to stay within the wafer of lucid air, holding his breath each time a disturbance enveloped him in the smothering lower reaches of the cloud. Even at floor level the air was now so polluted as to abrade the tissue of his lungs, and he began a slow steady coughing. A lurid redness began to pulse in his vision.

Hasson blinked his eyes, squinting ahead through his two-dimensional continuum, making the belated discovery that the shifting red light was not a subjective phenomenon, but something that had its origins in the external world. Driven by impulses beyond his understanding, he squirmed forward, towards the source of the intermittent radiance. Eventually, an incalculable time later, he found himself lying on the shore of a circular lake.

He shook his head, trying to restore a sense of scale, the ability to relate to his environment.

What he was seeing was not a lake, not a pond, not a pool. It was . . . an elevator shaft.

Hasson looked down into the shaft—narrowing his eyes into slits to combat a hot upward draught—into its dwindling, receding telescopic sections, the alternating concentric rings of darkness and orange fire which had at their distant hub a small, black, unwinking eye.

The eye hypnotised him, beguiled him, seduced him.

Hasson broke free of it with an effort and turned his attention to the massy oblong block of the power pack still clutched in his left hand. He rolled onto his side and, working with the languid precision of a man in a trance, fitted the unit into the vacant retaining clips, noting as he did so that the metal case had a heat scar which meant it could have been grazed by the thermal cutter which had ended Barry Lutze's life. He wiped a dark and tacky residue off the two electrical connectors and locked them into the adjoining counter-gravity generator on his belt. Nothing remained for him to do now but to rotate the master control, thus energising the flight system, and step into the waiting elevator shaft and fall to safety. Hasson mused briefly, making himself ready.

It was, of course, an unorthodox means of taking to the air—one not recommended by any of the numerous manuals on techniques of personal flight. The CG field would be disrupted and unable to take effect within the confines of the elevator shaft, which meant he would fall fourteen storeys and more, passing well clear of the underside of the hotel, before any lift would be generated. The total free drop would be something like sixty metres, a distance he would cover in approximately four seconds, making a small allowance for air resistance. It was, granted, an unpleasant and uncomfortable way to embark on a flight, the sort of thing which might upset a nervous person or a raw beginner, but it was nothing, nothing at all, to an experienced air cop who in the course of an arrest had once plunged *three thousand metres* . . .

Hasson rotated the master control on his belt panel—and smiled a tremulous, disbelieving smile when he saw that the function light had not begun to glow. The message, if he accepted it, was that his counter-gravity harness was inoperative, that he had no chance of escape.

I'll tell you three things this might mean, he said to himself, dulling his reactions with textbook pedantry. *Then I'll tell you the one thing it DOES mean.*

It might mean you're getting no power, but that isn't definite. Current could be coming through, but the microprocessor in the monitor circuits may have decided that the power pack is not in the peak of condition. The microprocessor doesn't seem to know what an emergency is—it treats every take-off as the beginning of an eight-hour demonstration flight.

It might mean that you damaged the CG generator when you hit that window frame down on the second floor, but that isn't too likely—those units are built to withstand a fair amount of abuse.

It might mean that the function light itself is broken—that's been known to happen, though not very often.

There was a louder, more immediate and more threatening rumble not far away, in the direction of the staircase he had recently vacated, and the ceiling of smoke became agitated, pushing down on him like a diaphragm. Still lying on his side, he drew his knees up and closed his eyes.

And the one thing it DOES mean—Rob, Mr. Hasson, sir—is that you would stay up here and suffocate rather than take that drop. Who could blame you? Who in his right mind would choose to fall fourteen stories through a blazing building . . . and come out of it into thin air higher than the Empire State building . . . with all that distance still below him, still to drop . . . without knowing whether his CG harness was going to work or not? It's impossible. Beyond reason. And yet . . . And yet . . .

Hasson stirred, moved closer to the grinning edge, and looked down into the descending and receding fiery circlets of the shaft. He looked into the black central disk—at the far side of which the world lay waiting—and understood that it was not an eye at all, that his father was not watching him, that nobody was watching him. He was alone. It was entirely up to him whether he chose to die, or to be born again.

He made the decision by relaxing his muscles, allowing himself to fall forward, giving himself up to a lazy dream-like tumble into the unknown.

Four seconds.

Measured by normal human time scales, four seconds is a very brief interval—but Hasson was receiving incomparably vivid sense impressions at a cinematic rate, and for him all clocks stopped and the heavens ceased to spin. He had ample time in which to glimpse the flaming battlefields of successive floors, to feel himself breast the battering sound waves of their passing, to endure the growing emptiness in his stomach which told him he was gathering speed in response to the earth's silent and deadly summons, to experience the alternation of light and shade, heat and comparative coolness, to think, to scheme, to dream, to scream . . .

And when, finally, in the murmurous, wind-rushing darkness—with the hotel receding above him like a black sun—he felt the counter-gravity harness begin to gather lift, to bring order into howling chaos, he truly had been born again.

CHAPTER 11

AL WERRY AND Henry Corzyn were buried in neighbouring graves on the sunlit, south-facing slope of a cemetery close to Tripletree.

Hasson, native of an island where cremation had long been compulsory, had never witnessed a traditional interment. The burial ceremonies he had seen portrayed in televised holoplays had prepared him for a surfeit of sombre emotion, but the actuality was strangely tranquil. There was a sense of rightness about the return to the earth which left him, if not comforted, in some measure reconciled to the facts of life and death.

Throughout the ceremony he remained apart from the main body of mourners, not wishing to make any statement about his relationship with Werry by joining any particular group. Sybil Werry, who had flown in from Vancouver, stood close to her son. She was a small dark woman, whose slightness of build made the fourteen-year-old beside her appear tall and unexpectedly mature. Theo Werry kept his head erect, making no attempt to hide his tears, following with slight movements of his sensor cane the final lowering of his father's coffin. Looking at the boy, Hasson could see clearly on his face the imprinted features of the man he was to become.

May Carpenter and her mother, discreetly veiled, formed part of a separate element containing Dr. Drew Collins and others who were strangers to Hasson. May and Ginny had moved out of the house a few hours before Sybil Werry's arrival and were staying in another part of Tripletree. Not far away from them stood the disparate figures of Victor Quigg and Oliver Fan, both scarcely recognisable when attired in formal black. Behind the knots of individuals, placing them in a common frame of reference, the city sparkled cleanly and uncaringly in the distance beneath the pastel traceries of its aerial highways. Hasson saw everything with an intensely detailed clarity which told him it was a scene he would revisit many times in memory.

As soon as he got back to the house he went to his room, which the sun on the drawn blinds had filled with parchment-coloured radiance. He laid out his belongings and, working with calm concentration, began packing them into a new set of flight panniers. There was insufficient room for everything that had been in his cases, but he had no hesitation in selecting the items he required and placing the others in a sprawling heap on the bed. He had been busy for about five minutes when he heard footsteps on the landing and Theo Werry entered the room. The boy stood for a moment, turning and tilting his sensor cane, then moved closer to Hasson.

"Are you really going, Rob?" he said, his face alert. "I mean now, this afternoon."

Hasson continued packing. "If I go now I can be on the west coast before dark."

"What about the trial? Aren't you supposed to wait around for that?"

"I've lost interest in trials," Hasson said. "I'm supposed to attend another one in England, and I've lost interest in that as well."

"They'll go looking for you."

"The world's a big place, Theo, and I'm going to gallop off in all directions." Hasson paused to make a proper acknowledgement of the boy's presence. "That's another line from Stephen Leacock."

Theo nodded and sat on the edge of the bed. "I'll get around to reading him some day."

"Sure you will." A sudden renewal of sympathy made Hasson wonder if he was being too self-centred. "Are you positive about not having those cataracts removed? Nobody would stop you having the operation done on one eye, anyway."

"I'm positive, thanks." Theo spoke with the voice of an adult. "I can wait a couple of years."

"If I thought you needed . . ."

"It's the least I can do." Theo smiled and stood up, releasing Hasson from self-imposed obligations. "I'm going away myself, you know. I talked it over with Mum last night and she says she has plenty of room for me in Vancouver."

"That's great," Hasson said awkwardly. "Listen, Theo, I'll go out there some time and see you. Okay?"

"It's fine with me." The boy smiled again, too polite to show his disbelief, shook hands with Hasson and left the room.

Hasson watched him depart, then returned to the task of loading his panniers with the essentials for a protracted solo flight. He had no fixed destination in mind—only an instinctive need to travel south and west, to begin his new life by pitting himself against the ancient curving vastness of the Pacific Ocean, to atone for the years he had wasted in parochialism and conformity by losing himself in domains where time and history had established no beachheads. A few minutes later—all preparations completed, all regrets put aside—he took off into the still blue air above Tripletree, and went for a long walk in the sky.

White Queen

GWYNETH JONES

Winner of the James Tiptree Jr Award, and nominated for the Arthur C. Clarke Award, Gwyneth Jones' *White Queen* depicts a deadly game of sex, politics and betrayal set against a backdrop of alien invasion.

'This is one of those rare books that stretches the intellect while it engages the heart. Satisfying as an adventure story, an unexpectedly moving love story, and as a believable glimpse of how things might be half a century from now, through its depictions of aliens, it may also make you look at human relationships a little differently – bound to be one of the key sf novels of this decade' – Lisa Tuttle, *Time Out*

'Seductively weird, depicting a future and a visitation, respectively grainy and bizarre in just the measure to convince, and populated by characters that live on in the mind long after the book's been put back on the shelf; a triumph of the depiction of otherness' – Iain Banks

0 575 05398 4   £3.99 net

Bill, The Galactic Hero on The Planet of Zombie Vampires

HARRY HARRISON AND JACK C. HALDEMAN II

Bill, The Galactic Hero – he's back, he's bad and about to meet the most hideous alien lifeform of his entire career. He'd do anything to save his skin without rocking the boat – but *mutiny*? On the *Bounty*?

The fourth in Harry Harrison's hilarious spoof sf series.

'A hangover cure for the jaded' – *The Guardian*

'Beyond satire into absolute farce with mayhem and merriness throughout' – *Science Fiction Chronicle*

0 575 05320 8   £3.99 net